Roxanne's Salvation

Book Two – The Mystical Healing Trilogy

By RP Mickelson

Filidh Publishing

Roxanne's Salvation
Book Two – The Mystical Healing Trilogy
By RP Mickelson
Copyright © 2024 by RP Mickelson.

ISBN: 978-1-998307-06-7

Published by Filidh Publishing Corp,
Victoria, British Columbia, Canada   filidhbooks.com

Cover Design: Danny Weeds
Cover Art by Zoe Duff and DALL-E software.

Other Books by RP Mickelson:

Stone House (2021)

Inspirational Short Stories (2023)

Lalita's Power (2023)

Preface

This novel is the second in a series of three works involving the power of mystical healing and reveals a new way to understand the universe. Despite the veil of suffering covering all aspects of modern civilization, there's a perfect harmony of peace, happiness and bliss lying at the core of Life. The existence of both Lalita Fitzgerald and Roxanne Wilson in this book exposes the key insights to spiritual living:

- Every aspect of life in the present moment is absolutely sacred.

- The transformation from suffering to ecstasy occurs when all the barriers to bliss are consciously removed.

- To abide knowingly in one's soul is where permanent happiness can be found.

Roxanne's Salvation is unsuitable for anyone younger than eighteen because it has mature themes and involves complex situations that only adults can fully understand. All the characters in the book are imaginary and bear no witness to anyone living or dead. Any likenesses to real people are purely coincidental.

RP   Mickelson
(email)   rick.mickelson@telus.net
July 8th, 2024

PART 1

The Peoples' Place

Chapter 1—<u>An Engagement</u>

If you looked at Roxanne Wilson's life from the outside you'd assume she lived an ordinary middle-class Canadian existence. But if you were ever fortunate enough to probe a little deeper, you'd learn she was extraordinarily complex. Her character was like a maze.

She was twenty-four years old, lived in one half of a two-bedroom duplex on Belmont Street in the Fernwood District of Victoria, BC, and worked part-time as a primary school teacher at Oaklands Elementary School. Actually, she shared a job with her friend and colleague Donalda Simpson, working from Monday morning until lunch on Wednesday.

She stood six feet tall, had long brown hair often tied in a tight bun just above her neck, dressed very professionally and was considered quite attractive by men. Her eyes were a deep green, like the color of a manicured golf course.

Roxanne was an *Anglican* and occasionally attended *St. Paul's Church* in Saanich. That was the church of her parents, and she'd been a congregant since she was baptized just after birth. At one point, she even taught Sunday school there for two years. Although she could never be considered *extremely pious*, she was moved, touched and inspired by the life of Christ and read a few verses of the *New Testament* on a daily basis. She was definitely a Christian in good standing despite the fact that she felt the official Anglican doctrine was dated, like an ancient bible.

"Jesus is my idea of a perfect human being; that's why I study His word daily," she told Donalda one day when they were having coffee in a dark corner of the Quadra Street Starbucks. "His life *truly* inspires me."

She was a very private person. Although she had many acquaintances, none knew her very well. Not even her fiancé, Brian Williams, understood her inner life, and there were many aspects of her that no one knew *anything* about.

For example, no one knew she *owned* the duplex where she lived or that she was heavily addicted to any form of cannabis that had a high THC content. No one knew she suffered from depression on a regular basis or that she wrote violent murder mysteries.

What people *did* know about her was that she was a law-abiding adult who held progressive political views and loved Taylor Swift's music. Also, anyone who had even minimal contact with her knew she was very compassionate. How else could you explain her habit of rising at 3 am twice a week to drive downtown and meet up with Reverend James Allen to distribute coffee and doughnuts to the hundreds of homeless folk who lived on the streets of Victoria?

"I grew up in the Uplands—a suburb where mostly rich people live," she told Brian. "I was an only child and had every conceivable *material* advantage. Most homeless people didn't have that advantage."

"Were your parents good to you?" asked her partner.

"No—my mom was a raving alcoholic who smoked, drank booze and watched TV all day long, and my dad, who was a successful building contractor, didn't spend any quality time with me. He bought me off with gifts. For my sixteenth birthday, he gave me a brand new red Toyota Corolla."

"What motivated you to get high marks and play on the high school basketball team?"

Roxanne frowned as she responded.

"Dad pressured me constantly to excel in school and sports, and I routinely did as he commanded. In fact, I always obeyed. Actually, I was afraid of him."

At her father's funeral, Roxanne shed many inauthentic crocodile tears and claimed she was too distraught to give the eulogy. She dressed in black, stood frozen at the grave site and talked to no one. Nevertheless, she *was* able to quite gracefully accept 1.8 million Canadian dollars and the duplex as her inheritance—facts she kept secret from everyone, including her beau.

"I think we should get married this summer," stated Brian rather enthusiastically at Easter, 2006. Roxanne's reply was telling.

"No, let's wait one more year until we've saved enough money to buy a condo."

"But we've already been engaged for two years!" he gasped. "Save for a condo? Surely, you inherited lots of money from your dad."

"We'll be married for a lifetime, so there's definitely no need to hurry. As for my dad—he didn't leave me a penny," she lied. "He bequeathed all his money to the law school at UVIC."

"Well, at least we could start living together. I'd like to move into your place because I hate being away from you."

"Yes, in time, darling—but I'm not quite ready for *that*," she responded.

A few days later, she met her friend Lucie Savarov for lunch at *Capone's Chicken Den* in Esquimalt. Lucie sang in the church choir, played the guitar and wrote her own songs.

"Glad you could make it today," Roxy said. "Let's take that table by the window."

"Sounds good," replied her friend.

"Our special today is a fresh chicken sandwich with onions and dill pickles," stated their waitress. "It's a two for the price of one deal."

"I'll order one," said Roxy.

"I'll have the other," added Lucie.

Between bites of her delicious sandwich, Roxy expanded on her prolonged engagement.

"Brian wants to get married this summer, but I put him off for another year," she related.

"Why?" replied Lucie.

"Because I'm still not sure about the relationship," answered Roxanne curtly.

"Do you love him?"

"Not particularly—but he's a good companion at times and when he's finished his accounting degree he'll definitely make good money."

"Why don't you love him?" asked her friend.

"Because he's pretty boring and just doesn't make me feel safe or protected. Also, he's a terrible lover with a small dong. We don't have sex very often." *I've never really loved anyone*, she thought. *But I better not mention **that**.*

"I think you should be totally honest with him and break it off," urged Lucie. "You can't marry someone you don't love!"

"Thanks for the advice. You might be right. I'll have to think about that," answered Roxy.

"Do you love Herman, Lucie?"

"Yes, totally—that's why I'm going to marry him. He's fabulous in bed, and we make love at least once every day. I'm his whenever he wants me."

Chapter 2—<u>Homelessness</u>

The next morning, Roxy was downtown on the streets at the crack of dawn with Reverend Allen. Her breath formed a steam cloud as she exited his van. The atmosphere felt cold, like a meat freezer. The first homeless person she saw was George Bacon, leaning against a telephone pole.

"Thanks for the coffee, ma'am—me was freezing and it warmed me up," George muttered. She noticed his blue hands shaking and his red nose running.

"You're most welcome, George. Would you like a doughnut?"

"Yeah, please," he moaned.

As she handed over a Tim Horton's double chocolate creamed treat, she took a closer look at him. He wore a black patch over his right eye and smelled of urine, like a piece of paper soaking in a dirty toilet. He was filthy, his two front teeth were missing, his clothes were tattered, and he wasn't wearing any shoes.

"I need a pair of boots. These socks don't keep the frost from bitin' my toes," he whined.

"I'll see what I can find," she answered. "I'll be back tomorrow with *something*. What kind of shoes do you wear?"

"Any kinda leather boot—sizes nine or ten."

After their rounds, Roxanne invited the priest to lunch at a nearby A & W. She opened up over thick bacon cheeseburgers, salty French fries, and hot black coffee.

"I'm depressed, Rev."

"Why?"

"The plight of these homeless people is wrong. Most of us have way more than we need, while our street brothers and sisters have *nothing*—not even a place to sleep at night. It's just not right."

"I'm a United Church priest who's been ministering to them for twenty-two years, and during that whole time, there've been tons of good intentions. But when it comes right down to it, the average person's not prepared to change their lifestyle or give anything up that'll help poor people. And that includes most of the church congregants I know."

"I'd like to donate $5000 to your ministry," she blurted out.

"Can you afford *that* much?"

"Yes—but keep it a secret," she answered wryly.

"You're most generous, Roxanne. That kind of money will help a lot of people, trust me."

"Thank you, Rev." He doesn't know it, but part of the reason for my gift is his mentorship, she thought. I trust him totally, *and he inspires me to do more for poor folks*. "It's the least I can do for him and his people."

"You might be able to get George a pair of boots from the *Thrift Shop* at Your Place, Roxy."

 "Maybe, but I'm sure my friend Lucie's boyfriend has a pair of old leather boots he never uses, and they might fit him."

"What a lucky coincidence that'd be," replied the minister.

"Yes," answered Roxanne.

Chapter 3—<u>A Depression</u>

While sitting alone that afternoon, an inner blackness took over her mind, so she called Ramón Perez—her drug supplier—the one who brought her the sticks of Columbia Gold she enjoyed at $100 a joint. She preferred going to him rather than some commercial outlet for grass because his dark, dirty character helped her maintain large doses of self-hatred.

I hate my life, she thought. *Brian's lack of passion drives me crazy, my job bores me, and I have no true friends. The only living thing I love is Menam, who is a Siamese cat. My whole life is meaningless.*

Ramón arrived at her door two hours later. She opened it a crack, just wide enough for him to pass three stogies through the open slit. She stared at his trimmed black beard. She felt his rough, magnetic virility while slipping him three crinkled one-hundred-dollar bills. Without saying a word she shut the door and backed up into the darkness that her home had become, eventually slipping heavily into her favorite reclining chair.

He's crude and corrupt, she thought. *What is it about him that attracts me? Maybe it's his virility and physical strength. Maybe it's because he's a Latino. I love his beard.*

She lit one of the joints and puffed deeply, holding her breath for a long time before exhaling. Soon her vision was blurred, the pain in her heart tamped-down and her body relaxed. She dozed off. The living room was thick with smoke, and stank like burning bits of cedar.

Once stoned, she drank a twenty-sixer of gin while eating a bowl of raw oatmeal smothered in yellow sultana raisins. Then she started to write. As the food was devoured, bits of cold porridge oozed from her lips, plopping onto the kitchen table. Still, in a daze, she picked up a thin, black ballpoint pen and started scribbling feverishly on a pad of foolscap. Invariably, she wrote about women who'd been savagely murdered. They were the heroines whose cases were never solved by the police.

Charlotte will be killed brutally with no clues left, she thought.

A real Charlotte actually lived in the other half of her duplex and was Roxanne's tenant. In the bizarre story that emerged, this naïve, innocent, indigenous woman was poisoned and stabbed repeatedly by Roxanne herself, who had morphed into a Russian spy sent directly over to Canada by Vladimir Putin. The death was to punish her for flirting with her boyfriend. And it was grotesque.

With the murder scene complete, she stopped writing and slumped back into her Lazy-Boy. Her heavy eyelids closed, and she sat there, visualizing the grisly crime scene and concentrating on all the gory details. Blood was splattered all over the walls, and Charlotte had been decapitated.

Two hours later she woke up and glanced groggily at the several pages of writing strewn all over her prized red and white Persian rug, the thick one with chariots and stallions on it. The one she'd bought at a market in Istanbul two years before.

All of a sudden, she was stricken with horror and a sense of dread. She didn't know whether the story was true or false.

Stumbling outside she banged hard on Charlotte Smith's front door. "Is anyone home?" she screamed. Finally, after what seemed like an eternity, it opened.

"I'm here; what's the matter?" muttered Charlotte with a puzzled look on her face.

"It's just me wondering if you're okay."

"Why wouldn't I be?"

"I just had an awful feeling about your safety, so I had to check." *She's in a very bad way*, thought Charlotte, *I better be nice to her.*

"Do you want a coffee?"

"Why not?" Roxanne blurted out loudly.

Once inside, she noticed a sparsely furnished living room leading to a galley kitchen full of spice plants, hanging fruit baskets and several lavender flowers. *I didn't know she was so good with vegetation,* mused Roxanne to herself. *This place smells nice.*

"Is your boyfriend here?"

"No, Roxy, he's on a naval exercise in the *Hawaiian Islands.*"

"That's good to know," she thought, forgetting that Charlotte had already told her about her boyfriend's deployment twice. Her tenant showed no signs of impatience with Roxy because she was a laid-back person and loved the conditions of low rent and excellent repair management. Since her boyfriend was away for months at a time, it helped to have a caring, understanding landlord.

On the way back to her place, walking across the porch, Roxanne noticed Menam sitting in the sun, purring contentedly. *My heart sings when I see her so happy*, she said to herself. Then she bent over and patted her cat tenderly.

Chapter 4—<u>A Proposal</u>

The next morning she was out again with the Reverend, dressed in an Inuit parka that had a mink collar. He was a man of infinite compassion and charisma and street people loved him.

"Here's a pair of German leather boots, George, size nine and a half," she told the vagabond. "They were owned by the brother of a good friend of mine who always buys high quality footwear. But he doesn't want them anymore."

George Bacon looked up at her through tears. He was still leaning against a telephone pole, shivering in the wind, shoeless, depressed and alone. Like a scarecrow in a barren winter garden.

"Oh my God—they beautiful," he said, slipping them on. "A perfect fit—you're so kind. Thank ya' and thank ya' friend."

"George, why are you crying?" she asked.

"My wife has diabetes, and we can't afford the medication. She's slowly dying."

"Can I speak with her?"

Getting up slowly, George said, "Follow me," as he limped away, using a crooked old oak cane to hold him up. Inside a makeshift plastic tent with two roof holes that let in the rain, Gloria lay in a tattered, zipperless sleeping bag. Roxanne saw black rings under puffy eyes inside a hollowed-out face of exhaustion. She bent down and touched Gloria's shoulders. They were cold. She was fifty-two years old, but the hard life of a former prostitute had taken its toll. Roxanne turned away from her shriveled body, looked up at George and spoke these words,

"I'll return later today with some insulin, George. Could you stay in the tent with her until I get back?"

"Yeah, of course I will," he moaned.

Somehow, the compassion in Roxanne's heart was unlocked and flowing outward. In that moment, she experienced Gloria's suffering as if it were her own. The barriers between her and a desperate woman suddenly broke down.

"You're going to be okay my dear," said Roxy. "All you need is a steady supply of insulin."

Through a medical connection at the Open Door, a local homeless resource center, Reverend Allen was able to secure a six-month supply of insulin for Gloria, which Roxanne took straight back to her. After injecting her with a shot of the much-needed drug, she showed Gloria how to administer the treatments. Soon the afflicted woman was feeling much better.

"You've saved my life today, Ms. Roxanne," she cried out unashamedly. "I'll never forget that."

"It was nothing, Gloria; it was just part of my job today. Please stay warm and let George look after you. You're going to be fine."

During lunch that day, Reverend Allen praised her and pointed out how compassionate she could be.

"Your sensitivity to Gloria was amazing, Roxanne. You have a real mission with my street people. As a matter of fact, I'd like to recommend you for my job. I'm going to retire in six weeks."

"Why do you think I'd be able to do *your* work?" She mused, taken aback.

"You're an ideal candidate—you're experienced, and you care passionately about the plight of our clients, and *they know it*. If I recommend you, the Board will hire you, guaranteed."

But I'm too busy writing a novel and planning a wedding, she thought.

"Let me think about it, Rev. I *am* a bit shocked and need to process this *slowly*. It's true the situation regarding destitute folks in our city speaks to me in a powerful way. Somehow, I want to make a difference in the whole problem of homelessness in this town. Just leave it with me. In the meantime, can I talk to you about a personal matter?"

"Why yes, of course," replied the minister.

"I'm engaged to a man I don't love. In fact, he drives me crazy, and I don't think marriage and family are my destiny. I was thinking about breaking the whole thing off, but he *really* loves me, wants to have kids with me and frequently acts completely dependent on my support. I'm worried he'll do something stupid if I dump him."

"I'm not one to give advice on marital matters, Roxy, but I *will* say this: it'd be cruel to marry a man you don't love. That wouldn't serve him or you—ever!"

"I'll have to meditate on that idea, Rev. Thanks for listening to me." *I trust this guy totally, and what he's saying makes sense,* she thought.

Chapter 5—<u>Ramon</u>

While writing at her desk the following Saturday night, there was a loud knock at her door. When she opened it, her Latino drug supplier Ramon's large muscular shape confronted her, and she immediately saw he was in bad shape—blood stains covering his dirty T-shirt.

"What happened?"

"Got into an argument with a couple of *gringos*—can I come in, *senora*?"

Reluctantly, Roxy opened the door.

"Let's smoke a *yerba* joint," he slurred.

"I don't really want to spend the money."

"This one's on the house, and it's really solid."

"Come in then, and let me clean you up first. Take off your shirt, Ramon," she ordered.

When she saw his black, hairy chest, she felt both repulsion and a puzzling attraction which she didn't understand. Was it because he was a fighter, a biker and a dangerous man? She carefully washed his cuts, sprayed them with hydrogen peroxide and then applied antiseptic Johnson and Johnson band-aids.

They each smoked a full marijuana cigarette, then started laughing uproariously and felt hungry. "You got any food around here, *amiga*?" he asked.

"Just a box of pitted prunes and some frozen vanilla yogurt ice cream," she replied.

Soon after that, they polished off the whole box of ice cream and a pound of prunes. Ramón then pulled a quart of Crown Royal out of his satchel, and they shared it. In short order, they polished off the whole bottle.

"I have to hide out tonight. Can you let me dormir here—sleep for the night?"

"I guess so," muttered Roxy.

The following morning at 4 am, she got up, glanced at the sleeping, naked body beside her and went straight to the bathroom. Her right thigh was throbbing, and her lower body ached, so she opened her kimono, exposing a bare leg that was blue with bruises. Vomiting into the toilet, she swore, then thought, *I'm going to apply for the Reverend's job.*

At a breakfast of dried white toast and black coffee, she informed Ramón her days of drug use were over.

"Our association has to end now because I won't be smoking any more dope," she told him. "And what happened last night can never happen again."

It took her a while to get him out of her apartment, but as soon as he left, she picked up Menam, petted her slowly, combed her hair, massaged her rook, then put her on her soft red sofa and stopped to listen to some loud purring. Then she sat down at her desk to compose an email to her fiancé. It read,

Dear Brian—

Our relationship has had some value for me in the past, but my life is about to change dramatically. I'm cancelling our wedding and breaking off the engagement because I'm taking Reverend Allen's job when he retires. It's a full-time commitment.

My one hope is that your life <u>without me</u> will be filled with happiness, joy, peace, and contentment—all aspects of a quality family life you could never have <u>with me</u>. You deserve that!

Roxanne

Shuffling through her novel, she felt sick again. Without a great deal of thought, she tossed the entire manuscript into a wastepaper basket.

Brian didn't take the break-up very well. He kept leaving emotional messages on Roxanne's cell phone—sobbing and begging for another chance. But her resolve was set, and there was no going back. Her ex-boyfriend spent six months in a mental institution, and Roxanne didn't visit him once. That was partly because she knew her presence would make him worse and partly because she was full of guilt over his reaction to the break-up. Despite the fact that she knew that ending the engagement was the right decision, she also realized that leaving him would cause Brian immense suffering. And it did. Just one day before his scheduled release, he jumped out a fifth-floor window early one morning with two chained bed sheets tied to his bare neck. Before the paramedics could get to him—he was gone— dangling in the wind for three hours before a psychiatric nurse coming into work found him.

Roxanne *did* go to his funeral and periodically laid a few red carnations on his tombstone. When she did so, it was impossible for her to avoid slipping into a dark depression. She might not have loved Brian, but she certainly cared about him. However, her life was getting so intense and demanding she didn't have time to linger in a state of melancholy. She kept extremely busy in her teaching job and expanding work with the homeless, and that process took her mind off personal problems. She was hoping that serving *others* would enable her to repress all her past traumas, addictions and bad memories because she was desperate to escape the past.

Brian's only living relative was his sister, Gertrude Williams, and she blamed her brother's demise on Roxanne. Unfortunately, she had schizophrenia, and her take on what happened to Brian was exceedingly distorted. Two weeks after the funeral, Roxanne received a very disturbing email from her. It read:

Bitch—

*I was the only one who visited your fiancé while he was locked up in a mental institution suffering from a broken heart **caused by you**. You killed my brother for no reason. Do ya' really think you're gonna get away with this?*

*He told me you **never** came to see him—not even once while he lay there shakin' after all the electric shocks drilled into his body. You abandoned him.*

*My sweet brother said your father was rich and for sure left you money when he died. **I want some of that money.** If you mail me a registered money order for $50,000, I'll go away—*

but if you don't, I'll keep torturing you. Don't forget to have it tracked by the post office.

GW
17—218 Gateway Road
Victoria   V8X 2Y7

This email upset Roxanne but she decided to ignore it. She knew Gertrude was mentally unbalanced and thought her threats would go away—if and when she got back on her medications. *She always acts like this when she's upset,* thought Roxy. In this way she misjudged the situation completely.

Chapter 6—<u>Rosa</u>

When Roxanne told James Allen, she'd apply for the job, he was ecstatic.

"I'm really tired of teaching, Rev. and need a change. I think I can do a good job. The situation of our homeless population drives me crazy and I want to do more to help, I really do," she said coolly.

"I'm so happy to hear that," he replied. "And I know you'll do a fabulous job but you don't have to apply—I've already received approval to offer you the job! It's yours."

Once she actually started the position, her routine was as predictable as clockwork. The full orientation took one month, and during that time, Reverend Allen trained her in every aspect of the vocation. He picked her up at 4:30 am every weekday morning, rain or shine. They went straight to Tim Horton's, had coffees then loaded up the padre's van with food and drinks paid for by Victoria's Your Place, a center for homeless clients. One cold October morning, two weeks before the Reverend retired, she began to open up to him.

"The plight of Jerry ripped my heart out yesterday Rev.—he was so wounded, so vulnerable, so hopeless."

"Jerry's a Songhees elder who fell on hard times and his life story is horrific. His mother was ripped on heroin during her entire pregnancy and his father was in jail on assault charges when he was born. During his childhood, he had to endure countless paternal beatings, so he ran away from home at the age of fifteen. His girlfriend was pregnant at the time and had Jerry's baby two months premature. However, soon after that, she eloped to Regina with his best friend, leaving the baby with him. Then his landlord evicted him on a cold November day because he was broke and couldn't make rent. Child protection services took the child away and he started living on the streets, addicted to coke and ecstasy."

I can relate to his addictions due to all the traumas in my past, she thought. *I too often feel an overwhelming desire for any substance that can take me away from my dark thoughts and feelings.* "Oh my God" moaned Roxanne laboriously, "Rev.— how can we help someone like Jerry?"

"Despite the fact that most of the large institutions in town— including churches—only pay lip service to the plight of the homeless, there are a few independent services that *can* help. But the most powerful agent in dealing with people like Jerry *is us*! We can make a big difference by simply caring about him, talking and listening to him *without judgment*, keeping him warm, feeding him hot coffee and delicious sandwiches and sometimes referring him to the right agency or process."

Roxanne noticed a family of four black crows on some icy telephone wires when they left the coffee house. Two of the birds were greedily gobbling up seeds they'd picked up in Centennial Square from two plastic buckets left out by Frank, a destitute hobo. The other two jet black crows were cawing loudly. It was eerie and made her feel something awful was about to happen. Below the birds on the street were several scantily clothed men huddled together desperately trying to keep warm under a damp, dirty sheet of brown canvas. There was frost on the statue of Sir John A. Macdonald beside them.

"Rev., can we go to into Christ Church Cathedral after lunch once our shift is over?"

"Yes, we certainly can—but why?"

"To pray," she replied calmly.

The cavernous cathedral was bathed in a profound silence, like the inside of an ancient Egyptian pyramid. But there was light streaming into it from twelve magnificent, colored stained-glass windows. The only congregant was a young woman covered by a bright red shawl, kneeling with her head bowed in the front pew. When she shut her prayer book the sound echoed throughout the building, resounding off the vaulted walls.

Roxanne sat down behind the praying lady and soon Reverend Allen joined her. Looking up, her breath was taken away. Hanging above the communion table was a life-sized oak figure of Christ with His heart open. He came alive for her in that moment and she visualized His blood dripping onto the church's massive golden pipe organ. Her eyes slammed shut.

"Jesus, help me minister to your people—the sick, the broken, the addicted and the lonely ones outside in the street," she muttered under her breath while sitting on a hard oak bench. Suddenly, a deep peace enveloped her and she felt a strong urge to kneel, which she did. In that position of humility and submission, she continued to pray, like a devoted nun.

"My Lord, I beseech You to send down your love upon the homeless in this city. Please guide me in how to help them. Your grace is my sufficiency in all things."

Roxanne prayed silently, in earnest, alongside the Reverend for over an hour. During her entire contemplation the woman in front of her knelt without moving a hair. Later in the day, while at coffee, she asked James,

"Rev., do you know the woman who was kneeling in front of us at the church?"

"Yes, I do," he replied. She's Rosa Devlin, a very devout Christian. When she comes in here, she prostrates herself in front of Jesus for up to four hours. People tell me she's a mystic healer."

"I saw that she was slowly turning a bright red rosary in her hands the whole time she prayed. Is that normal?"

"Yes, for her, it is," replied the father calmly and slowly.

"I'd like to meet her; Rev. Would that be possible?"

"Yes, it would. She goes to Sonya's Teahouse every day after church. Tomorrow, I'll introduce you to her."

On the day Roxanne met Rosa, it was snowing lightly, and the Christmas tree outside Sonya's was white, its branches dusted with glistening snowflakes. The pious woman was quietly sipping a cup of steaming, non-decaffeinated green tea in a corner of the shop. The Reverend walked meditatively up to her and said, "Hello Rosa, how are you today?"

"I'm just fine, as usual," she replied, smiling, "and feeling very grateful to be alive. The world is full of exquisite blessings today."

"Well, I have a friend with me today who's helping with my work and she'd like to meet you. Her name is Roxanne. Actually, she's training to take over my job."

"Hi Rosa, I've seen you at Christ Church Cathedral," opened Roxanne.

"Yes, that's right—I go there often—it's nice to meet you," she answered respectfully.

"Well, I'll leave you two alone to talk, as I must be going now," the priest added.

Roxanne was shocked to see how young and beautiful Rosa was. Her smiling face had classical features like a Greek goddess, and she had thick blonde hair that reached all the way down to her waist. Her skin was flawless and her big, bright blue eyes were penetrating and full of wisdom. *Can't be more than twenty-five years old*, she thought.

"Roxanne, would you like some tea? There's a whole pot here and I can ask for an extra cup."

"Why yes, that'd be nice," she replied cheerfully. Sitting down, she continued, "I wanted to meet you after watching you at the Anglican Church downtown. Reverend Allen says you ardently pray there frequently."

"Yes, that's true! I love listening to Jesus."

"Is it also true that you can cure people with medical problems?"

"Well, sometimes…if a person truly wants to be healed I'll pray for them."

"Are your prayers answered?"

"If the patient's sincere, they often are."

"What's the secret of how to pray properly to create healings?" inquired Roxanne.

"There *is* no secret. I just close my eyes, go into a profound state of silence and wait for the Lord to respond. Once the mirage of human life evaporates, He always does."

"Could you pray for me?"

"Do you need healing?"

"Yes, I really do. I have so many problems to fix," blurted out Roxanne.

"Do you want to be free of all your problems?"

"Yes, yes…"

"What seems to be the matter?"

"I crave marijuana when I see the suffering of my homeless clients. I get depressed. I'm attracted to crazy men. I imagine gruesome murders then want to write about them—and I frequently contemplate suicide."

Rosa looked deep into Roxanne's eyes. Her compassion poured into them before she shut her own eyes briefly and went totally silent. "If you come to my place tomorrow afternoon I'll work with you," said Rosa. "Can you do that?"

"Yes, I can—what time?"

"Right after tea-time at Sonya's—let's say 1 pm. My address is 8-725 Pembroke Avenue. That's in Fernwood."

"Oh that's convenient—you live in the same neighborhood as me," noted Roxanne.

Chapter 7—<u>A Healing</u>

The next day, Roxanne found her way to Rosa's home through a series of quaint lanes that wound around massive oak trees over forty feet tall. They were mostly covered in vines of ivy that were a deep green color, like fresh seaweed. Her apartment was very small—five hundred square feet at the most. She stood in front of Rosa's front door for a moment, staring at the stone building in front of her, deep in thought. Then she knocked quietly three times on the thick oak door before it opened slowly.

"Come in, Roxanne, and welcome to my humble abode," said Rosa as her guest stepped through the front door and entered her suite. It was modest and very simple—immaculately clean with very little furniture—only a single bed, a small table, a wicker chair, a rocker, a chrome microwave and a mini stainless steel fridge. One whole wall was lined with a variety of spiritual books and another had shelves containing knitting supplies and many bright colored bundles of wool. A large bi-fold pink closet door sat near the edge of Rosa's tiny kitchen. Roxanne immediately noticed the calming scent of a large jasmine plant right below the front room window.

There was Christian meditation music playing softly in the background. Rosa's environment made Roxanne feel calm, relaxed and peaceful. After a short period of small talk, Rosa asked her,

"Would you like some healing energy now?

"Why yes I would—most definitely," she responded hopefully.

"Then have that seat, hold my hands and become perfectly still."

Roxanne moved into the assigned chair and placed all her fingers into two hands that had soft, silken fingers and nails that were clean and manicured. The hands were warm and welcoming.

"Now close your eyes and go within, Roxanne."

They sat silently for quite awhile during a period where Roxy lost complete track of time until Rosa finally released her hands.

"Praying is really very simple. It's all about falling into the center of your being and listening intently for the voice of Jesus. That's all you need to do to help yourself or anyone else who suffers. Remember—we don't do any healing ourselves—but if our consciousness is raised high enough, healing happens without us. Our Savior does all the work."

Roxanne was by this time completely relaxed, enveloped in a quiet peace. She felt calm and aware of everything that moved or made a sound. It was an ecstatic feeling. Space and time had disappeared. For some time, no thoughts entered Roxanne's mind. Finally, she stood up and slowly found her balance.

"Thank you Rosa," she said while putting on her heavy coat. "I feel so much better already."

"You're most welcome, my love. Come back anytime."

When she met Reverend Allen the next morning, he asked her,

"Did you meet with Rosa?"

"Yes, I did."

"Was her interview helpful?"

"Rev., I had a wonderful time with her and it had a powerful impact on me. A peace came over me after she showed me how to pray that can't be described with words. All of life seemed very sacred at that moment. Since then, my constant sense of dread seems to be losing its power over me, and the desire for marijuana has evaporated."

"That's excellent," exclaimed James. "The rumors that Rosa can heal may be true then…"

"It certainly feels like it but time will tell. Nevertheless, I think her impact on people will be very different than yours, James."

"How do you mean?"

"She does all her healing alone with Jesus—she doesn't actually go into the world to help anyone in person."

"Well I think that's wonderful—but it's only half the solution. The other half is action."

"Please elaborate."

"I mean an authentic Christian has to get their hands dirty. Meeting the homeless where they are—advising them, assisting them and caring for them. That's where the rubber hits the road and *real* healing takes place. Remember the words of our Lord—

Jesus asked Peter, "Do you love me?"

Peter answered, "Yes Lord, you know I love you."

Jesus then asked Peter again, twice, "Do you love me?" Peter angrily answers,

"Yes Lord, you know I love you." Jesus then replies,

"Go out and feed my sheep."

At that point, Roxanne looked closely at the Reverend standing up. He was a tall, handsome man with a ramrod straight back, clear eyes and a voice full of conviction.

"You inspire me, sir," she whispered. "And that's why you're one of my most powerful mentors."

Chapter 8—<u>Prayer</u>

Once the Reverend had fully retired, Roxanne threw herself wholeheartedly into the work. At first, her will and determination forced an understanding of the homeless folks she met daily. She came from a background of privilege and prejudice so it was difficult to relate to the physical suffering of those on the lowest rung of society. However, in a psychological way, she fully comprehended the grasp addictions can have on a person's life. And if someone has no worldly resources to help them given the high cost of living today, they inevitably become homeless. *There, but by the grace of God, go I,* she often thought.

The latent racism that lay repressed deep in Roxanne's unconscious also had to be addressed and this particularly applied to assisting indigenous people. The Reverend had gone to great lengths educating her about the Sixties Scoop and the Residential School Debacles. Through that process, she learned about the horrific cultural genocide experienced by First Nations band members in an age gone by. It was a very ugly story.

On her second day on the job she encountered William Lincoln, originally from Greenville, BC. He was on heroin when she first met him.

"I'm glad you came this morning Roxanne," he told her, "Because today will be the last one I have in this world. Do you see the dirty needle in my belt?"

"Yes I do Billy."

"Well, it's full of over-proof liquid heroin, and it's going into my arm *very soon*."

Clearly, he does intend to kill himself, she thought.

"Why would you do that Bill?"

"They took me away from my parents and two brothers when I was five years old, ma'am," he started to say, shaking all over and waving his fist in the air. "I had to go to a private Anglican school to be "civilized". That meant getting up at 5 am every day to milk cows, promising to never speak my native tongue, enduring repeated sexual abuses and worshipping a foreign God. The only thing that takes me away from my past is heroin, cheap wine or whiskey. I'm sick and tired of my life. That's why."

I've got to keep him talking, thought Roxanne nervously, *and try to offer him hope where I can*, as she stared at the tears flowing down William's face. At times her heart was pounding when she was with him because there really *was* no hope in his case. He was full of a bitter anger that had penetrated his soul and he'd come to the end of his tether.

"I had to endure sexual abuses from my father," she blurted out spontaneously, surprised that she'd uttered those repressed words to a virtual stranger, "and it still torments me—but I've been able to move on—and you can too! Now listen to me—if there was a way for you to be completely healed would you give it a chance?" she inquired,

"Yeah, but that ain't gonna' happen."

After listening to William and letting him vent for over two hours, she went directly to the cathedral and started to pray, *in earnest.* She stayed on her knees for one hour and thirty nine minutes, like a novice nun seeking holy acceptance.

"Can I join you for tea today, Rosa?" Roxanne asked after their contemplations ended and she saw the religious walk out of church.

"Why most certainly, my dear sister—let's go to Sonya's," she responded.

In the weeks and months that followed, Rosa and Roxanne started to become close friends. Their relationship was based on a mutual desire to heal the sick, enable the poor and cure the wounded. They both interpreted this vocation as one that acted on the essential elements of Christ's teaching.

"Can I ask you to pray for William Lincoln, Rosa? He's close to killing himself due to depression, alcoholism and lack of care."

"Does he want to get healthy again?"

"Yes," responded Roxanne.

"Then I *will* pray for him."

"Thank you, my friend, I feel confident that praying will have positive results."

In time, under tutelage from Rosa, Roxanne slowly began to understand how mystic healing could take place for the homeless. First, it was important that her clients *wanted* that healing, *requested* it and *let it happen.* But she was also a disciple of Reverend James and, from him, learned how to minister daily *in a physical way* to the homeless people of Victoria. When she was working with the disenfranchised, her own past traumas, addictions and character flaws were suppressed and temporarily forgotten. Every client she saw made her realize how lucky she was to be able to function effectively in the world despite her many character flaws, hang-ups and idiosyncrasies.

Chapter 9—<u>Death</u>

When Roxanne came home after work the next day she was shocked by the sight of her front door. On it was nailed Menam, stiff as a board. Her mouth was wide open revealing a tortured look with fresh blood slowly coming out of it onto the porch; drip, drip, drip. There were two spikes holding her to the wood—one punched through her throat and another penetrating her long black tail. Under her body, taped to the wall, was a blood-soaked note which read.

Mail me the money—**now**. GW

Falling to the ground, Roxy covered her face with both hands and wailed hysterically until Charlotte came out of her suite and put both her arms around her. "Who would do such a despicable thing?" moaned the tenant, as soon as she noticed the hanging cat.

"A terrorist," blubbered Roxy, tears streaming down her face like a fast-flowing waterfall.

It took two days for Roxanne to calm down after experiencing the horror of her beloved cat's death. During that time she was mercifully supported by her neighbor, Reverend Allen and Rosa.

"You need to take a picture of this right now and then call the police Roxanne," stated the minister. "This isn't just a prank, it's a criminal assault and the perpetrator must be found and made to bear accountability for it."

"I will then Rev., as soon as my nerves get stable. In the meantime, would you do a funeral for Menam?"

"If that's what you want Roxy, I'll do it," he nonchalantly responded.

The next weekend, Reverend Allen showed up in full United Church regalia and Roxanne, followed by Charlotte and Rosa carried a small pine box into the gardens behind her home. The procession stopped at what was a raised bed of rich soil meant for tomatoes in the summer. They then slowly lowered Menam into a prepared hole in the dirt. Tears flowed continuously from all who were present.

"We're gathered together today to honor the life of a wonderful friend," Allen intoned into the gloomy silence. "May her soul find peace in the next world."

After the garden was once again leveled and a prominent wooden cross placed over the site, the four attendees trudged slowly into Roxy's kitchen for light refreshments. These included tuna sandwiches, cold apple juice boxes and a large, iced Angel Food cake with a Siamese cat depicted on it. Her name was etched onto the cake with black and white icing.

The police were helpful and it didn't take them long to find the culprit. However, they told Roxanne there wasn't much they could do other than place a restraining order on Ms. Gertrude Williams—which they did.

During the Christmas holidays that year, Roxanne visited the local SPCA and came away with a pure white, fluffy, spayed, and inoculated Persian cat. It was happy in Roxanne's home but often kept her awake at night with extraordinarily loud noises, so she named him *Snore.*

Chapter 10—<u>A Relapse</u>

Roxanne prayed hard for Lincoln in the way Rosa had instructed her. As time went on she was glad to find out that he *didn't* kill himself, his health *was* improving and the insulin made a big difference in the life of his wife. But she was still distressed that he kept drinking hard liquor and injecting both himself and his wife with small doses of pure heroin. Dread and sadness began to seep into her mind and she felt a strange craving for marijuana but somehow resisted smoking it.

With just three days left before Christmas she went into her back yard, stood by Menam's cross and burst into tears. She stared at the grave and longed to hold her Siamese cat again. *I miss her so much*, she thought. Later that night she drank two glasses of undiluted Johnny Walker before grabbing her cell phone and dialing Ramon's number.

"Hi, it's me," she sighed. "Can you come over tonight?"

"Hola Rox—do you want to fumar with me—I've got a fresh supply of great Columbian Gold pot?"

"Yes."

Ramon arrived on his reconditioned 1996 Harley two hours later. It was windy and raining hard as he walked up Roxanne's curvy stone path but he was only wearing a muscle shirt, a pair of tight leather pants and big logger boots. His black beard was trimmed, and his mustache clipped, giving him a heroic look, like Sylvester Stallone in Rambo. *I'd hate to get into a fistfight with him*, she thought, watching him trudge up the walkway. But later, after smoking a full joint, Roxy began to relax. She then felt vulnerable and really wanted to communicate with someone.

"My ex-boyfriend's sister, Gert Williams, killed Menam and nailed her to my front door," she blurted out.

"Dios mio—why'd she do that?" he asked.

"Because she blames me for Brian's suicide."

"That's dumb," muttered Ramon. 'He was an idiot gozque from the beginning."

"Yeah and she also wrote me a note demanding fifty thousand dollars. If she doesn't get it by the end of this week, I'll be facing more punishment."

"Did you call el policia?"

"Yes I did," answered Roxanne abruptly. "They put a restraining order on her but said they couldn't do anything more at this time."

"What does this perra look like?"

"A scary woman—she's got a long nose, a pock-marked face, big ears and a bright blue skeleton tattooed onto her neck. She looks like a Halloween witch."

"Where does she live?" continued Ramon.

"In trailer #54 at the Sandringham RV Park in Langford."

"Roxy—don't worry about el problema of Gerty Williams anymore—I'll take care of her."

During a long bout of rough physicality, Roxanne didn't sleep for even five minutes. Her body fluctuated between ecstasy and pain all night long. In the morning, she was exhausted. Her thighs and back were very sore but she felt content, like a starving refugee who'd just eaten a delicious feast. While Ramon slept she brewed a pot of hot coffee then nibbled on a piece of dry Melba toast slathered with crunchy-style peanut butter. Somehow, she was able to ignore Snore's presence, curled up sleeping by the front door, even though he was snoring loudly.

I've got to go to church today, she thought. *I need to pray for clarity.* She was conflicted about how the night had unfolded but one very good outcome did come as a result of Ramon's visit. She was never bothered by Gertrude Williams again.

He sure knows how to take care of business, she thought. *And he's got guts.*

Chapter 11—St. Paul's

As she got further into her new work with the homeless, Roxanne returned to her original Anglican congregation at St. Paul's in Saanichton, BC. She now attended every Sunday service and the Wednesday evening Bible Study.

St. Paul's had two large, separate buildings. One was what the minister called 'the main church' which had a long white steeple, beautifully stained-glass windows picturing all the Stations of the Cross, sixty hard oak benches, a large communion table with creamy-green tapestry cloth, a massive organ with twenty-two pipes and a seated section at the front for the choir. In the basement was a classroom for Sunday school, a full kitchen and a compact seating area with tables, chairs and bulletin boards. The other structure was a cavernous church hall with one hundred stacked chairs, a stage, a kitchen and two washrooms.

The larger building was modern and operated traditional services for a largely middle-class, white, aging congregation, while the smaller one was a church hall mainly used by the Church Army, populated by three First Nations Bands. The Church Army was led by four indigenous lay readers who managed the Sunday gathering in an unpredictable way. The actual service generally started when enough people had arrived and began with native spiritual music by whoever brought instruments. Depending on the occasion, or the mood of the leaders, the meeting could last anywhere from two hours to three days. Sometimes, in the summer months, the whole congregation would embark on a sing-a-long, dug-out-canoe trip that paddled all the way along the sea coast to Duncan. There was little or no contact between the two congregations at St. Paul's.

The main church's priest was Reverend William I. Jennings and his curate was Samantha Cartwright. Father Jennings ran the church with authority and Ms. Cartwright always demurred to him even though her religious training had been far more thorough than his. Roxanne loved the liturgy, the hymns, the prayers and the communion process at Reverend Jennings's Sunday event. But for her there was a great deal missing at St. Paul's because she took the teachings of Jesus very seriously, based on her prolific readings of the New Testament. There she learned about the life of a Man who hung out with prostitutes, lepers, thieves, political radicals and social outcasts. He was not a conventional person in any way and constantly rebelled against the established religious traditions of His day.

At St. Paul's there was no radicalism. Its congregants were well-off middle-class people who conformed to all the prevailing social and cultural mores, like robots programmed to follow instructions. Reverend Jennings consistently preached against feminist themes, gay rights and pre-marital sex. "Sex is only appropriate in marriage and for the creation of children," he used to say. Homeless folks were not actually welcome at this church. His service began at precisely 11 am and ended, after an excruciatingly long sermon at 12:15 precisely. After a 45-minute break for coffee, tea and cookies at the social time downstairs, the church was routinely shuttered until Wednesday's Bible Study. And that Study, led by the deacon Ms. Cartwright, promoted a very literal interpretation of the Bible complete with heavy moral overtones, hell fire for transgressions and guilt-inducing exhortations. For those reasons, Roxanne asked for a formal interview with the minister. After arriving at his executive office, she knocked loudly on a door that was partially open.

"Do come in Miss Wilson," Jennings answered in a monotone voice. He sounded like an answering machine on low volume.

He was sitting at a long mahogany desk in a swivel chair glancing casually at his personal computer. His office was immaculately clean but looked sterile to Roxanne. Jennings felt no need to get up to greet his visitor and glanced at her over pince-nez spectacles.

"Have a seat, Miss Wilson," he said, pointing to a plain metal chair in front of him. How can I help you today?"

The minister was a tall, thin man in a gray suit with a white priestly collar. His face was thin, and his complexion was pasty white, like a ghost's. He looked tired, irritated, and bored.

"Thanks for agreeing to meet with me to discuss a proposal which I've outlined in this notebook," she said, sliding a duo-tang slowly across the desk into his scrawny hands and thinking that his long fingernails needed to be cut. "As you know, I work closely with the homeless in Victoria and minister to them daily by bringing coffee, sandwiches, clothes, medicines and blankets to them. I also refer out to several agencies and services in town. But Father, these people are hungry most of the time and I'd like to create a soup kitchen and food bank at our church to help the homeless in *this* community and other underserved Island locales. It's a much needed program—all outlined in my thirty two page typed-proposal along with all the costs and fundraising strategies."

Jennings coughed softly, paused for a long time, then frowned at his guest. "That's an interesting idea Roxanne but I have a few questions for you."

"Let me try to answer them then."

"How would you get these clients to our church from their encampments all over the city?"

"We'd have to purchase a second hand van, sir," replied Roxanne.

"And how would you deal with the complaints we'd get from all our neighbors?"

"How do you mean, Father?"

"This same idea was floated five years ago, and a questionnaire was sent out to all the homeowners in our district. The results were unanimous—don't bring any homeless people into our neighborhood or our protests will be vigorous and unending until your church goes down. That's why we had to drop that idea quickly."

"But, sir, I've been reading the New Testament and it's clear to me that Jesus was inclined to heal the sick, minister to the poor and take care of the downtrodden. He even performed miracles to transform those who flocked to Him for help. He never let the opinions of naysayers stop Him."

"Those were different times my dear. Nevertheless I'll present this proposal to the Board next month and we'll see what kind of reaction we get. We should know the answer in a couple of months. I appreciate all the work you've done putting this together, Roxanne. Now if you don't mind I'm going to have to excuse myself because I've got another appointment in five minutes."

Roxanne was not shocked by Reverend Jennings' brusqueness or his insensitive reaction to her ideas, but she was extremely disappointed. Seven weeks later, her angst deepened when the board unanimously voted down her proposal.

I've got to talk to Reverend Allen about this, she thought.

Chapter 12—<u>Your Place</u>

"Reverend Allen, is there any way you can join me tomorrow morning on the street? There are a few things I'd like to discuss with you."

"Roxy, I'm busy tomorrow but can we meet on Wednesday morning? Could that work?" replied James into his cell phone enthusiastically.

"Yes, that'll be fine."

"Let's meet at London Fish & Chips on Broad, it's pretty central."

"Okay, great," she responded.

Broad Street was full of homeless people during the night because many of the storefronts there were deeply recessed, which gave them some protection against the elements. At that time, Spike was sleeping on the doorstep of London Fish & Chips. When James and Roxanne walked up to him, he was lying outside his wet sleeping bag, shivering and whimpering. It had been raining very hard all night long.

"Rev—so good to see you again—I missed you bad," he muttered. "Can you help me, I know I'm dyin'?"

Spike's face was emaciated, dirty and caked with dry blood.

"God loves you Spikey and so do we," countered the minister. "We'll be back at 9 am to take you to Your Place and get you cleaned up. You need medical attention, a hot shower and some dry clothes."

"God love ya', bro'," cried out Spike.

Roxy and James pulled up to Your Place in the Reverend's rusty, white van precisely at 9:30 am. Spike lay shivering stiffly in the back of the vehicle.

Your Place was a community center for the homeless in Victoria. It fed a nourishing daily lunch to just over three hundred destitute folks wandering in from the boulevards of Pandora Street. It also had hot showers, a food bank, a large closet full of used clothing, a games room, a dental chair, a nursing station and eight administration offices.

They were able to extricate Spike from the van and, by each holding an arm, got him into the facility. Once there, Jill Ornstein, the resident RN, took him into her area and laid him out on a clean mobile bed. Its outside metal railings were down.

Soon she came back into the lobby and said, "After your friend has a shower, I'll need to clean up the cuts all over his body—some of which are infected."

"We'll be back this afternoon to check on him," answered Reverend James.

By this time the Reverend had decided to stay with Roxy until her shift ended. When it did, they went for drinks at Sonya's. Over cups of hot Brazilian coffee and sticky cinnamon buns, thick with sugary sweet vanilla icing, Roxy began to open up.

"I'm really depressed about the way St. Paul's is being run, James."

"What are your concerns?" he responded.

The main church is a beautiful building replete with every possible attribute that could satisfy a lively, committed Christian community. But it's only open two days a week for very short periods of time."

"Can you be more specific?" he parried.

"The Sunday service lasts exactly seventy-five minutes, followed by a short social time downstairs. Most of the mass involves a long sermon which has very little to do with the teachings of Jesus. It always involves moral exhortations against pre-marital sex, homosexuality, women's equality, abortion and social protests. This *does not* reflect my understanding of the New Testament. Jesus roamed freely around the countryside healing people non-judgmentally, performing miracles demonstrating the power of God and protesting the rigid religious beliefs of His time. This is so frustrating—our church is like a social club not a place that facilitates transformational living."

"Have you met with Father Jennings?"

"Yes I have. We had a brief meeting in which I proposed the creation of a soup kitchen and food bank at St. Paul's. He thought that was a bad idea."

"Well, you could start your own soup kitchen y'know," added the padre rather confidently.

"How could I do that?"

"Start by praying about it and then begin a fundraising campaign like the ones I used to run. Did you know I raised over half a million dollars to get the Your Place Building Fund started?"

"No I did not. That's very impressive and I'd like to find out exactly how you did that," answered Roxanne.

"And I'd be more than happy to explain how to do it," replied the minister.

On their way home they stopped briefly at Your Place to see Spike.

"Spike's already gone," Jill told them. "He left here over an hour ago—wearing dry, clean clothes, carrying a bag full of food and showing off a clean body with all his wounds treated."

"I wonder where he went?" asked Roxanne.

"Back to London Fish and Chips, no doubt," added Father James. "This is what I call a *vicious cycle*. He'll be back here at Your Place in a few days needing more care and attention because he's got both drug and mental problems."

When she got home and readied for bed, Roxanne's mind was preoccupied with the disturbing notion that the homeless people in her city were caught in a *vicious cycle*.

"Maybe I can change that situation, Snore," she whispered to her cat, whose loud purring began to calm her nerves slowly. Snore, I'm going to pick the Rev.'s brain on how to fundraise over the next month." And true to her word, that's exactly what she did.

Chapter 13—<u>Bertrand</u>

Roxanne kept praying on a daily basis—sometimes for up to ninety minutes at a time. She'd start most of her prayers appealing to Jesus directly—

"Dear Lord, King of the Universe, please help me see the light. I beg You to show me how to deliver Your power to St. Paul's."

Even after her most fervent sessions of contemplation, she never heard the voice of Jesus. One Sunday afternoon, she spent all of it in deep meditation at Rosa's apartment.

"I keep asking Jesus to help me resolve the stalemate at church, Rosa," she said in exasperation when they'd finished their supplications. "But He doesn't respond."

"Roxanne—if you're sincere, He *will* answer you—I promise. Be patient. Jesus speaks to people in many different ways."

That night, Roxanne fell into a deep sleep that lasted nine uninterrupted hours, much longer than usual. During that time, she had a very vivid dream—one that she actually remembered the next day.

She was inside a large center for the homeless and it was magnificent. On the second floor were sixty rooms for women, each fitted with a clean bed, small window, plywood dresser and Gideon Bible. The same configuration of rooms existed on the third floor for men. On each of those levels was a massive community washroom with ten showers and five toilets. On the main floor was a cafeteria that served nutritious food at cost, three large classrooms fitted with every conceivable learning device, a massive warehouse and a thrift shop full of clothes, toys and furniture.

That kind of Healing Center would be perfect for all the homeless people of Victoria, she thought lying wide awake in bed the next morning—*now how can I make that dream become a reality?"*

Not knowing how to start was a problem but now Roxanne had an unshakable conviction: Jesus wants me to make this happen. *This is how He speaks to me*, she thought, *in dreams*!

A few days later she remembered her father's best friend. He'd been a successful clothier and international fashion designer who created, manufactured and sold women's clothing internationally. At one point he had two hundred retail stores in North America. He was also a deacon at St. Paul's. His name was Jonas Bertrand and he'd been retired for five years. During Roxanne's childhood, Mr. Bertrand was often seen at family gatherings and always took the time to develop a special bond with her. For example, he always attended her birthday parties giving lavish gifts to what he considered was one of his *special friends*. Since he had no children of his own, Bertrand treated Roxanne as if she were his own daughter. When she turned sixteen he bought her a 2006 Toyota Corolla CE. She loved that vehicle, drove it for three years and never forgot Mr. Bertrand's generosity.

She felt inspired now to ask him for suggestions on a business plan and budget for what she was going to name, The Peoples' Place. *Perhaps he might become my first donor*, she thought.

Bertrand lived in a seaside mansion on Beach Drive, an exclusive enclave for the wealthy citizens of Victoria. His gated property was located on two acres of gardens, stately trees and included a luxurious beach house right on the ocean. The home had six ornate bedrooms, five full bathrooms, a plant-filled conservatory, a games room, an indoor swimming pool, a luxurious kitchen with two gas stoves, a grill, a large microwave oven, two stainless steel fridges, a stand-up freezer and a cooled wine cellar.

"Hello, Jonas, it's Roxanne Wilson," she said on her first cell phone call to him. How are you?" she asked as calmly as she could, despite her nervousness.

"Well, Roxanne, so very good to hear from you. I'm just fine."

"I'm really sorry about your wife's passing, Jonas, and I apologize for not going to the funeral. I've just been so busy with my new job."

"I can understand that, so don't worry about it. Lenore was not really acting as my wife for many years. In the end, dementia got in the way of *real* marriage. I'm coping alright—considering the fact I now have no family whatsoever."

 "Actually, Jonas, I have a favor to ask you. Can I come to your home to discuss it?"

"It must be a complex matter if you need to visit me. What's the problem?"

"I'm developing a detailed strategy for an enormous homeless shelter, training center and food source, and I need a viable business plan to show the government and the banks. I thought you might be able to give me some suggestions."

"I'd love to help Roxy. Why don't you come by tomorrow evening for supper?"

"That'd be fine," she replied. "What time?"

"Come by at 7 pm, and you don't need to bring anything."

"See you then, Jonas."

When Roxanne showed up at Bertrand's residence, the gate was already open in anticipation of her arrival. When she knocked on his front door, the portly butler, Paul Stricker, opened it.

"Welcome Miss Wilson," he said, "Come in and have a seat right over there in the living room," he muttered, breathing heavily and pointing her in the right direction. "What would you like to drink?"

"Do you have any sweet red wine?" she replied.

"Yes ma'am, coming right up."

Once Roxanne sat down, she looked around and was amazed by what she saw. Over the massive natural gas fireplace hung a self-portrait of Jonas Bertrand, which must have been ten feet tall. Its oil colors were thick, bawdy and poorly coordinated, like graffiti on a warehouse wall in the slums. That particular painting was only one of seven other works of art in oil that adorned the vaulted walls, some of which were impressive. She recognized an original work of Emily

Carr and was certain the picture of a colorful, four-dimensional mask was one of Picasso's finest.

After drinking half a glass of Pinot Marseilles, she began to relax just before Jonas approached the luxurious black leather armchair she was sinking into.

"Hello, Roxanne, welcome to my home," he said. "Why, you're looking gorgeous tonight," he added while staring at her just a bit too long.

"Thank you, but all my flaws are covered by clothing. At any rate, your estate is magnificent. I can't believe how majestic it is—like an aristocrat's palace from ages past."

"I do like nice things and a home with lots of space."

"Do you live all alone now?" asked Roxanne.

"Just me and two staff—that's all. Now—please tell me about your business plan."

Roxy then proceeded to share with Bertrand her vision of a massive homeless housing and training center that would be named The Peoples' Place.

"You're very animated when you talk about this project, Roxanne, which makes it very interesting to me. You've obviously got a lot of energy for this project."

"Thank you," she responded. "I believe my vision is divinely inspired and know you'll be able to relate to that, being as you're a devout Christian and all. Would you be willing to help finance this project, Jonas?"

"This undertaking looks very exciting to me. I have one question: Isn't there already a center for the homeless downtown?"

"Yes, Jonas, there is, but Your Place has a limited scope. It has no housing, no vocational training programs, and only serves the homeless in three south island municipalities. It's not set up to help enough destitute people these days. My Center will serve people from all over the island and *have* training programs and housing. And this is only Phase 1 of my overall plan. I also want to buy farmland and expand by putting another center on North Island."

"I can understand that, Roxy. Give me one week to read your entire proposal, and then let's meet again. Can you come back for dinner next Saturday evening?" he asked.

"Yes, I can, and I will," she answered with conviction.

Chapter 14—<u>Rosa's Talents</u>

As time went on, Roxanne came to view Rosa as an authentic *kindred spirit*. They often met in the afternoons at Sonya's for hot green tea and conversation. Rosa was quiet, introverted, wise and somewhat detached, like a magical, wise owl. When she *did* speak, her words were powerful—partly because she always looked directly into the eyes of her listeners and partly because her vocabulary was rich. She focused her total concentration on what was being said. Since she was completely non-judgmental, Roxanne was at ease sharing her most intimate thoughts and secrets.

One day in mid-January when the weather was extremely frigid she was invited to Rosa's for a lunch of croissants served with Brie cheese, olive oil mayonnaise, sea salt and hot house tomatoes. Her apartment had a fiery portable electric heater sitting in one of its corners, so the room felt cozy.

"This food's exquisite, Rosa, did you make the buns?"

"Yes, I did; croissants and crusty bread are my specialties."

"That's amazing."

It was then that Roxy became aware of Rosa's passion for knitting. "I love your sweater—it's gorgeous with so many integrated and brilliant colors. Where on earth did you buy it?"

"Actually, I made it myself," replied Rosa. "I'm a knitter."

"That's astounding—you're so talented."

"Would you like to see my current stock?" asked Rosa.

"Yes, of course."

The pink closet door was opened, revealing eight shelves of perfectly woven bulky sweaters.

"Oh my Lord, they're exquisite!"

"Thank you—why don't you try one on? Here, I'll get you a medium."

Rosa then helped her friend put on a white sweater full of bright red roses, which fit like a glove.

"How much would a garment like this cost?" asked Roxy.

"Three hundred dollars, but I'm going to give this one to you."

"You can't do that," gasped Roxanne.

"Yes, I most definitely can; consider it yours."

"Thank you so very much, my dear friend. I'll treasure this for the rest of my life. Do you sell many of these?"

"I turn over about five a week—at local sales, craft fairs, retail consignments and orders from regular customers. It's my primary source of income. After morning prayers, I generally knit in my rocking chair for four or five hours. For me it's a form of meditation.

"That's incredible!" exclaimed Roxanne. "You're a very gifted person."

"Let's put that notion aside and pray for a few minutes."

"Sounds like a wonderful idea," replied Roxanne, bowing her head, closing her eyes and going deep within herself.

Chapter 15—<u>Planning</u>

The week passed quickly, and it seemed like before she could blink, Roxanne was back at the Bertrand residence. After enduring the usual introductory small talk and imbibing a glass of wine, she was invited by the butler to sit at a dark-stained mahogany table that was twelve feet long and four feet wide and had tall-backed chairs. On it sat a golden candelabrum holding twelve lit candles. She was sitting to the right of Bertrand, who was at the head of the table. He wore a dark red smock with a yellow daffodil pattern covering a starched white shirt and black bow tie. Roxanne noticed his tightly trimmed, gray mustache and smelled his potent aftershave.

She thought *his face looks thin and pinched, and he smells funny.*

Mr. Stricker served five courses: yam fries with an onion-garlic dip, broiled Pacific salmon smattered in fresh lemon juice, hot, crusty French bread, a Caesar salad with croutons, and pitted dates from Lebanon for dessert. During dinner, Bertrand talked endlessly about facts and ideas that held no interest for Roxanne. His mind had a dry, technical quality, and his discussions went into too much trivial detail. And he wasn't a particularly good listener.

Will he ever get to the business plan? She thought.

Finally, she interrupted and blurted out, "That's nice, Jonas, but did you get time to read my proposal?" After a long silence, he replied,

"Yes, I did, Roxanne—the executive summary and all the other thirty-five pages."

"What did you think?"

"I liked it, a lot. In fact, I wouldn't make a single change—including your expansion plans into farming and another center up the island. After consulting with my accountant, I'm estimating a budget of three million dollars for your first center."

"Wow—that much?" winced Roxanne.

"Yes and that includes leasing a large warehouse I own at a price significantly below market rates."

"What would the warehouse be for?"

"It's big enough to be converted into the entire training and homeless shelter. As it happens, this particular building has three floors."

"Are you prepared to pay for the entire project Jonas?"

"No, I'm not. But I *have* come up with a way to finance it."

"How would that be?" inquired Roxanne eagerly.

"I'm willing to make a cash donation of 1.5 million dollars and am confident we can raise half a million from private donors I know and specific provincial government funding programs I'm aware of. I have several connections to key personnel at the Ministry of Welfare and Social Development.

"Sounds fantastic, but your plan still leaves us a million short."

"True, but that's where you come in. I happen to know exactly how much you inherited from your father. I also know he bequeathed you your current duplex. Roxanne—you *can* afford it. We can make this happen!"

"Let me get this straight—you're asking me to contribute 1 million dollars?" gasped Roxanne.

"Yes, I am," whispered Bertrand.

After ten minutes of an awkward silence, he asked her,

"Roxanne, why are you so quiet all of a sudden?"

"You've given me a great deal to think about Jonas. I do want to thank you for putting all this together."

"Thank you—but there's one more consideration, one more piece to complete the puzzle, so to speak. In order to move forward with the project, I'm going to request you live with me—as my wife—for two years. That would include fulfilling all the duties normally expected in a marriage, including sleeping in my bed every night. But it wouldn't include having any intimacy with another man during that year."

"Oh my God Jonas—you're thirty two years older than me!"

"Which would make life very exciting for both of us," he added with a smirk on his face.

"Are you aware that I get up at 5 am five days a week to go to my job?" replied Roxanne flatly.

"No but that won't be a problem at all—I'm an early riser too!"

At that point in the discussion, Roxanne looked exhausted. Her eyes started to close and she began to sway slightly in her seat.

"Stricker," called out Bertrand, "Get some smelling salts, my guest's going to faint!"

She didn't faint but Roxy laid her head down on a nearby couch and asked Stricker to use a fan to cool her down. Twenty minutes later she sat back up and composed herself.

"My dear friend, I've got enormous respect and admiration for you—but I can't love you in that way."

"What way is that?"

"I can't love you as a wife."

"That's not a problem for me at all," replied Bertrand. "This would be a strictly a business arrangement—besides, the deal only requires your services for two years."

Roxanne then stood up, asked Stricker for her coat and headed for the front door. Just before walking out of Bertrand's house, she turned and said,

"You've certainly given me a lot to think about. I'll need time to pray about this and talk to my mentors. However, I *will* get back to you regarding the proposal you've put forward—and that's a promise."

"By when?" he asked.

"The end of February."

"But that's six weeks away, Roxanne."

"I know," she responded. "I'm asking you to be patient."

Chapter 16—<u>Arlene</u>

The next morning at 5:37 am, Roxanne encountered Arlene McNab, a fifty-one-year-old alcoholic ex-prostitute. Arlene was leaning up against a barren maple tree. It was cold.

"Why are you moaning, Arlene?"

"My left arm hurts and both my feet are frozen."

Roxy pulled up the left arm of her damp Cowichan Indian sweater and stared at a gaping wound full of maggots. Then she glanced at Arlene's feet and noticed the derelict was shoeless and shaking uncontrollably. Roxy immediately dialed 911 on her cell phone then put her arm around the waif, trying to warm her up.

"I need an ambulance quickly—at the corner of Johnson and Broad. A woman's dying in my arms," she coughed into the phone.

Forty minutes later, Arlene was lying in a hospital bed waiting for several test results.

"I'll be back in later today to check on you Arlene."

"Thank ya' for holding me and helpin' me," slobbered the wounded woman.

Walking briskly back to Your Place on Pandora Street, Roxy felt sad but inspired by her own actions. *I'd never have touched a woman like Angie six months ago,* she thought. *I'd have considered her too dirty.*

Later in the day, she saw Rosa at Sonya's.

"Can I join you for tea, Rosa?"

"Why of course—have a seat."

"Good I've got to talk to you about something crazy."

"What is it?"

"In my pursuit of funding for The Peoples' Place, I met up with a retired businessman who's an old family friend. Actually, he was my father's best pal when he was alive and he's extremely wealthy. This guy has offered to fully support my dream project for the homeless financially, emotionally and strategically on two conditions: (1) that I myself put up a million dollars and (2) that I live with him *as his wife* for two years."

Rosa fell silent and looked into Roxanne's eyes in a penetrating way. "Can you afford a million dollars?"

"Yes, but please keep that confidential."

"Do you love this person?" she asked after a long pause.

"No."

"Could you ever love him?"

"Not as his wife, Rosa. He's thirty-two years older than me, and he's not my type!"

"Then there's only one solution. You've got to go to Jesus until He makes your future abundantly clear. You'll never resolve this matter satisfactorily unless He speaks to you. Let's start the process by praying right now."

At that point, they both closed their eyes while sitting in the restaurant chairs and entered a state of absolute silence for ten minutes. After that, an exquisite peace descended upon both of them.

"I feel more focused now," whispered Roxanne.

"Me too," replied Rosa.

After she left Rosa, Roxy went directly to the Jubilee Hospital. There she found Arlene in Room 415 South. The patient was hooked up to an IV with her left arm fully bandaged. She looked like an Egyptian mummy but her face was a rosy color and she was smiling.

"Ms. Wilson, I'm so glad to see ya'. Could you hug me?"

"Of course my dear," Roxanne answered while placing her arms around Angie's shoulders, closing her eyes and squeezing tightly. *I can feel the totality of her pain*, she thought.

"Nobody touch me for seven years," sobbed Angie. "I been too filthy, too sick."

"How's your arm?"

"The pain's gone."

"How about your feet?"

"They warm and treated for infection."

"You'll get through this, Arlene—you're tough. I'll be back to see you tomorrow."

Roxanne poured herself a stiff gin and tonic on the rocks when she got home then sat down and fell into deep thought. She was full of inner conflict.

Becoming Bertrand's wife is immoral, it's no better than prostitution, she thought. *What am I sacrificing to do this?*

She dozed off for a few minutes then got up and poured herself another drink. *But on the other hand I'm not doing this for me. The Peoples' Place will make life better for hundreds of homeless people and besides, I'm convinced Jesus wants me to build this Center. I can do this, I've got guts.*

After a third drink Roxanne fell into a deep sleep and didn't wake up for twelve hours.

Chapter 17—Another Dream

That very night, Roxanne had a vivid dream. She was working in a thriving training shelter for homeless people. Her third-floor office door had the following words emblazoned on it:

Roxanne Wilson
President & CEO

In the dream, she was taking Reverend Allen on a tour of the facility. It all seemed so real to her. She showed him the forty single rooms on the third floor and the forty-one on the second. Central to each floor was a spacious bathroom with eight toilets, twelve showers, sixteen sinks and four changing cubicles. On the main floor she walked the Reverend through a cafeteria serving delicious meals *at cost* all staffed by formerly homeless, but current students training to be cooks. There was also a thrift store, two large classrooms stocked with brand-new computers, desks, pull-down screens and a carpentry shop. The entire building was full of formerly destitute people who were now busy, productive and happy.

She woke up with a start when Snore jumped on her bed and started licking her left cheek.

"Snore, it's settled, Jesus does want me to build The Peoples' Place!"

Snore just sat there purring, contentedly licking her lips and whiskers with long, pink tongue.

I've got to write down every detail that occurred in this dream before I forget anything, she thought. *It's just the way Jesus wants it. Then I've got to meet with the Reverend.*

She found James at Our Place later that afternoon. He was a visiting lecturer there putting on a workshop called—*How to Prepare for a Job Interview.* She waited until he'd finished then approached him outside the small classroom as he left it.

"Can we go for coffee, Rev.?"

"Yes, of course—what's going on?"

"I've got to discuss something awesome, but bizarre with you."

"Let's go around the block then—to Tim Horton's," said the Reverend.

When they got to the Johnson Street eatery, Roxy dropped four loonies into a shivering beggar's baseball cap who was standing in the street outside. She recognized him. It was Tony John, the one-eyed ukulele player.

"Keep playing, Tony," she called out enthusiastically. "I love those Bob Dylan songs of the sixties."

Then she went inside and ordered a medium black coffee and a heated cheese scone with two slabs of butter and a package of strawberry jam. Reverend Allen followed her to a table with a small, steaming hot chocolate in his hand. It had whipped cream on it. They sat down.

"You're not going to believe this but I've received support for every aspect of my dream project. You were right, fund raising can work!"

"From who Roxy?"

"Jonas Bertrand, a very wealthy businessman. When my dad was alive he was his best friend."

"That's wonderful news, so what's the problem?"

"In order to move forward, Bertrand wants me to contribute a million dollars of my own money to the building fund and live as his wife for two whole years."

"Oh my Lord," winced James. "What are you going to do?"

"Rev., Jesus has spoken to me through a dream. He wants me to do this."

"Well if He supports the plan then so do I."

On her way home Roxanne went back to the hospital and was surprised to see Arlene sitting in the Sun Room reading a Bible.

"Arlene, you look happy and healthy. How are you feeling?"

"The best—haven't felt this good fa' twenty years."

Coincidently, Nurse Sylvia Jenkins, a tall and imposing RN just happened to be aiding another patient nearby. She dropped her current task and walked briskly over to Roxanne.

"Your client's recovering nicely but I must tell you what the surgeon told me. Had she arrived a day later, Arlene's left arm would have been amputated. You did a great service bringing her here when you did."

"Thank you Sylvia," replied Roxy, glancing at her name tag, "You've just made my day. Now—when will the patient be released?"

"We're thinking tomorrow morning. Does she have any family members who could pick her up?"

"No, but don't worry, I'll be here to get her as soon as you call me. My cell number is 250-788-4275."

"That's good to know. Can you be here by 10 am?"

"Yes, I can," responded Roxanne.

Now I've got to get home to write a letter to Bertrand, she thought

Chapter 18—<u>The Letter</u>

As soon as she got home, Roxy poured herself a Bacardi and coke then sat down at her desk with a real sense of resolve. Her letter was short and simply stated the facts:

February 2nd, 2007

Mr. Bertrand—

After conferring with my closest friends and praying deeply, I've decided to accept your proposal for a two year term starting on April 2nd, 2007. In addition to the specifics of your contract, I further request:

1. *A private office of my own, and*
2. *A new vehicle licensed and insured in my name for my exclusive use during the years in question.*

Sincerely,

Roxanne Joan Wilson
(email) rjw17@telus.net

This letter was placed in a large envelope, registered at the Tillicum Road Post Office and mailed the very next day. Exactly six days later, she received a reply.

It read:

February 8th

Dear Roxanne—

I'm delighted that you've decided to accept all the terms of the contract and I look forward to welcoming you into my home next month.

An architect, a general contractor and an accountant will be hired before the middle of February. Each will receive precise instructions in their areas of expertise based on your exact plans for The Peoples' Place. I've already received positive responses from three private donors.

You'll have exclusive access to an office on the main floor of my home, equipped with a desk, a computer system and all the office supplies you'll require. A brand new Toyota Corolla will be parked in my garage—waiting for your arrival. It'll be yours to use for the entire twenty-four months.

If you have any questions pertaining to our arrangement, please email them to me at your earliest convenience.

Most sincerely,

JR Bertrand
jonasrb@shaw.ca

Chapter 19—<u>Loneliness</u>

The next morning Roxanne was on the job bright and early at 5:15. The temperature was mild, but it was raining. Her first stop was Tim Horton's on Johnson Street. Tony was standing in his usual spot with a soiled New York Yankee baseball cap turned upside down in front of him. There were two quarters and a nickel in the hat. He was soaking wet, wearing a red acrylic sweater heavy with water and he was humming and shivering.

"It's awfully early to be standing here playing Bob Marley music on a mouth organ Tony. How long have you been here?"

"Since 2 am—couldn't sleep last night," he moaned—while humming and shivering.

"Where were you *trying* to sleep?"

"In that dumpster over there," he moaned hoarsely while pointing to the container.

"Tony—don't you know how dangerous that is? A garbage truck could have squashed you in a flash."

"Those trucks ain't comin' on Saturday nights," he moaned, shivering.

"Are you hungry?"

"Yeah—haven't eaten in two days."

It's so strange, thought Roxy. *Tony's freezing and I can feel the cold in his bones as if it were in my own body—but I've got a fur parka on and I'm sweating.*

"Come into the coffee shop with me and I'll buy you breakfast," stated Roxanne.

"For real?"

"For real—and you can get whatever you want."

Tony ordered two toasted breakfast bagels, two hash browns, two strawberry-filled, cream doughnuts, six chocolate timbits and a extra large hot coffee with two sugars and three creams. When the food came he gobbled it all down in under five minutes.

"Wow, you *were* hungry," laughed his care giver.

"Yeah—but is that coffee all you goin' have?"

"Yes," answered Roxy. "I had breakfast at home this morning. But never mind that. How are you doing these days?"

"Bad, real bad."

"Why?"

"It's been two years since I lost my janitor's job and haven't found work since. Nobody'll hire me."

"I'm sorry to hear that Tony."

"And my ex-wife killed herself last week by overdosin' on smack and me two daughters are goin' crazy. I wasn't talking to the woman any more but she *was* a good mom in her day. Look at me right foot—it's gone black! May have to have it amputated the doc says—if my diabetes don't get fixed soon."

"I'm so sorry to hear that too, Tony."

"It's okay I can handle it. The only thing me can't handle is the loneliness."

"How do you mean? She asked."

"Nobody cares if I live or die. Nobody talks to me. I'm all alone," he sobbed as tears started streaming down his face.

"I know that feeling Tony, I know it well. Can I give you a hug?"

As they embraced, Roxanne lost herself. The boundaries separating her from Tony collapsed. She let go completely and fell into the space. The peace enveloping her left only when a terrifying thought popped into her head--*I have to become a frigid wife in two days.*

"I've got to go now, Tony," she told him, breaking free of the hug.

"You's a saint Rox an I luv 'ya," murmured the homeless man.

Chapter 20—Paradise

On Saturday, April 7th, 2007, Roxanne closed up her half of the duplex, loaned Snore to her tenant, got into a Yellow Bird Taxi and was driven to Jonas Bertrand's mansion. Three large purple suitcases in the trunk went with her. She was feeling depressed and sick to the stomach. Her head ached. She closed her eyes and prayed. *Jesus—I'm doing this for You. Please help me get through this period in my life.*

As per a pre-arrangement, the gates at Bertrand's property were open when she arrived so the taxi passed through them moving quickly before Roxy asked the driver to slow down. When the cab stopped she noticed a brand new, shiny red Toyota Corolla CE parked by the front door. *I think that's going to be my car for awhile,* she thought.

Jonas was standing on the gray-tiled front porch beside a palm tree waving to her, like a friendly fox waving its tail.

"Welcome to paradise," he yelled, saluting her before she paid the driver and moved away from the taxi. "Stricker will take the luggage and put it in your office on the first floor," said Bertrand. "You can take your time putting all your stuff away. In the meantime, let's celebrate your arrival with some vintage wine. I just happen to have a bottle of 1947 Sauterne in my cellar."

Over time, Roxanne was pleasantly surprised to learn that her experience of life in *paradise* was not going to be as horrific as imagined. Bertrand treated her with respect and admiration from the beginning and was true to his word about The Peoples' Place. He took an authentic interest in this endeavor and turned out to be an excellent project manager. On that very first day their conversation centered on Roxanne's vision for the homeless people of Victoria.

"You'll be pleased to hear I've got *all* the anticipated donations secured and I've set up a bank account that already has two million dollars in it. Once I deposit your cheque, all the funding will be in place," he told her matter-of-factly.

"Oh my, that's just wonderful news Jonas—I'm very impressed," responded Roxanne with enthusiasm.

"Thank you. An architect's been hired and her blue prints are now ready for your perusal. The entire design is based exactly on the specific requirements outlined in your proposal."

"When can the actual construction begin?" Asked Roxy.

"As soon as you sign off on the plan, my dear."

"That's fantastic. I'll start studying the drawings tonight after supper."

"A good idea," replied Bertrand, "And as far as meals go, Stricker is my official chef and serves supper every night at 6 pm. If you have any special food requests let him know one week in advance. My kitchen is continually stocked with nutritious, wholesome groceries and you're welcome to eat any time you wish. You're on your own for breakfast and lunch."

"Thank you so much!"

Despite Bertrand's positive qualities and behaviors, Roxanne *did* have to endure what were, for her, a few 'irritations'.

He was meticulous about every detail involving The Peoples' Place but then again he was meticulous about everything. For example, he was a cleanliness freak. The slightest object or substance, such as a piece of hair that he thought out of place, immediately disappeared or was thrown away. He tended to talk incessantly about matters which were of no interest to Roxanne and he wasn't a good listener. His voice was affected to the point of being effeminate and he had a slight case of bad breath.

Roxanne did everything she could to limit her availability to Bertrand in bed—getting up early, often pretending to be asleep, sometimes spending the whole night on a sofa in her office and feigning overwork or illness when absolutely necessary. The horror of actual physical intimacy with him was seldom experienced because Bertrand had an enlarged prostate. That meant he was only ever able to participate in anything sexual after he'd taken two blue pills. Strangely, it was only ever attempted after he'd seen any kind of female nudity on TV. He did put his arm around her body sometimes, trying to force a hug, but she got used to it and trained herself to fall asleep whenever *that* happened.

Despite these problems, she actually started to become quite fond of Jonas and all he was doing to make her dream for the homeless come true. She also came to love swimming in his Olympic Pool every evening, drinking very expensive wines and being served like a queen by Stricker—despite the fact that these lifestyle perks were experiences in stark contrast to those available to her homeless clients.

"You know, I'm actually a very lonely man," stated Bertrand at dinner one evening.

"I'm surprised to hear that," replied Roxy. "You have every possible advantage in life and many people and friends surrounding you all the time."

"Yes that's true, but I don't have anyone who really knows me or actually cares whether I live or die. I have no kindred spirits in my life."

I've heard that emotion somewhere else, thought Roxanne. *Maybe all this wealth doesn't really make that much of a difference?*

By the first of May construction of The Peoples' Place was fully underway. Roxanne toured the emerging facility every day after work. She frequently invited Reverend Allen and Rosa to the building site to inspect the ongoing progress and they were always both very impressed.

Chapter 21—<u>Prison</u>

As life continued with Bertrand, Roxy was gradually learning how to deal with the man's irritations but the luxuries afforded her living with him were definitely enticing and counterbalanced the problems. She loved the exquisite cuisine, having full access to his kitchen and driving her brand new Toyota. One day in early May she noticed a message left on her voicemail. It said,

"Rox—I'm el carcela at the Wilkinson Road Jail. Can you visit me this Sunday, between 2 and 4 pm? You'll have one hour."

Oh no, she thought. *Why is Ramon contacting me now?* Strangely despite all the bad memories she had about Ramon, she missed him. *Why would he be in jail?* She wondered.

By the following Sunday she'd applied for, and been granted, a visitation pass. Between the hours of 3 to 4 pm they met in a small, barren anti-room that only had two dilapidated metal chairs in it and a small plastic table. The space was drab and had no windows. It was also stuffy and dimly lit with one forty watt bulb. An armed sheriff was present the whole time. The scene reminded Roxanne of a second-rate prison scene in a low budget Texas detective movie.

"You look fantastic Ramon," she gasped. "I love your hair short and you look handsome without a beard." She was also taken aback by his pumped-up biceps and significant weight loss.

"Thanks Rox. I'm feeling bueno," he replied.

"Why are you in here?" she asked.

"Got busted for trafficking and, since it was my first offence, the judge gave me two damn years less a day. With bueno behavior I'll be out in nineteen months. Then—probation for twelve months."

"How are you being treated here?"

"Malo, very bad—But I'm six months into a welding program and use the one-bike gym every day. I also been reading— four volumes of Encyclopedia Britannica done, only twenty more to go."

"Wow, that sounds amazing—I'm truly impressed."

"Rox—I decided to turn mi vida around, get clean, find a real job, contact my family when I get out and hopefully see more of you! Maybe we could become better amigos.

"That sounds great Ramon, truly remarkable. I congratulate you."

"Your hour's up," gruffly stated the obese sheriff, speaking with a particularly cold, harsh voice. Roxy noticed that he was coughing, breathing heavily and walking bow-legged.

"Okay sir, I'll leave now," said Roxanne. "But can I give my friend a hug on the way out?"

"Make it quick," snapped the sweating guard.

When she embraced her old friend, a warm current of electricity flowed throughout her entire body. She held him for as long as she could.

He's become a very attractive man with tons of charisma, she thought.

"Bye Ramon—I'll be back next Sunday," she whispered passionately into his left ear.

Thereafter, Roxanne spent one hour every Sunday with her former drug supplier.

Chapter 22—<u>Progress</u>

By the 1st of July, building progress on the Peoples' Place was making astonishing progress. The entire warehouse had been framed and the basic electrical and plumbing work was finished.

"At this rate we should be open to the public by Thanksgiving, my dear," Bertrand told Roxanne at supper one night.

"That's fantastic Jonas and I appreciate being given the task of hiring all the staff and designing their job descriptions. I also accept the candidates you've selected for the Board of Directors."

The truth of the matter was that Bertrand and Roxanne were working as a well-oiled machine on their project. It became clear that Roxanne was going to be in charge of the daily operations and the actual design of the Center was following her instructions down to the smallest detail. Bertrand handled all the legal requirements, the funding and money supply, the hiring of construction employees and the designing of a constitution. He'd recommended two of his close friends for the Board—Ron Gillespie—an architect friend who designed his mansion and Michael Dalton—the Deputy Minister of Welfare and Social Development. Roxanne and Reverend Allen were to become the fourth and fifth members of the Board.

Roxanne was experiencing real passion and joy as the summer months unfolded. Her relationship with Ramon was deepening and she remained close to both her spiritual mentors—Rosa and Reverend Allen. Bertrand knew nothing about Roxanne's developing relationship with Ramon.

"My parole officer has offered me a day pass on Labor Day, Rox," said Ramon on Sunday. "Can we spend it together?"

"I'd love that Ramon. I was planning to go to the Saanichton Fair on that day. You could join me if you want. It's a country fair in Saanichton that's been happening for one hundred thirty-seven years. They have a midway, craft sales, animal displays, continual live music, vegetable contests, lots of confectionaries and real horse shows."

"Yeah, yeah bueno!" answered the Latino.

"Do you mind if Rosa joins us?"

"No problemo—as long as you're there I'll be feliz—which means *very* happy." he added, smiling.

"It's a deal," added Roxanne. "You seem to be using your time in prison well, my friend."

"Haven't felt this good in ten years and next month I've been accepted into a sweat lodge retreat with fifteen other prisoners. It's supposed to help us clean out all our really malo stuff—all the bad things in our head."

"That sounds wonderful, Ramon. Let's hope it helps you."

Chapter 23—<u>Fernandez</u>

During the time Ramon was in jail, the Program Co-Ordinator at the Vancouver Island Regional Correctional Center at Wilkinson Road was Juanita Fernandez. Her close friends called her Jenny. She'd worked very hard to achieve that position having attained a PhD in Criminal Justice from the University of British Columbia. Her previous job involved a twelve-year stint as a prison guard at the Islas Marias maximum security penal colony in Mexico. Originally, her passport was processed as a student visa but while attending school in Canada she applied for, and received, landed immigrant status that was valid for five years. That allowed her to obtain employment at the Wilkinson Road Jail. One of her most important roles there was to manage the personal and social development of the inmates. That's how she came to meet Lalita Fitzgerald.

Gloria Felltham, one of Jenny's best friends at UBC, had attended a six day Sweat Lodge Retreat at the Surrey Native Friendship Center and raved about it.

"You've got to do this Retreat Jenny—the facilitator's a mystical healer. You won't believe this but it's true: she cured the torn meniscus in my knee without surgery, medicines or doctors. Now I can run again and play tennis—all thanks to her. Not only that, but after the Retreat my clinical depression disappeared and so did the arthritis in my back. All this was a miracle."

"Do you think any of the prisoners at Wilkinson would benefit from taking it?" asked Jenny.

"I absolutely do," replied Gloria enthusiastically, "Every last one of them would be completely transformed. I can guarantee it."

"Then I'll have to do it first," answered Juanita Fernandez, "Just to check it out."

Six weeks later she was enrolled in the Retreat and during the process met Lalita, the facilitator. This was a woman unlike any other she'd ever met. All ten of the Retreat participants were seated in a classroom when Ms. Fitzgerald entered the room to give her introduction. She was tall—very tall, perhaps six foot two and walked in slow motion. She had long black hair to match the color of her penetrating eyes. Her energy was overpowering like she'd just swallowed a meteorite and her face shone with compassion. However, she spoke very slowly, mindfully, carefully. And she was a woman of very few words. Her attention when it focused was like a laser beam.

"Welcome to your Retreat. I'm happy you're all here. Over the next week we'll remove all the energy blocks that are preventing you from realizing your true destiny. Don't doubt that for a minute. Now, please close your eyes for a short meditation and listen carefully to the meditation music.

Five minutes later she resumed,

"Sweat Lodge Retreats are sacred purification events. The steam from hot rocks will penetrate an enclosed space where you'll be sitting after fasting for twenty-four hours. I'll then lead you in visualizations and other practices designed to release all your past traumas. This is the way you'll recover authentic power. Please proceed to the longhouse outside and prepare to fast, chant and pray." Her voice had a magnetic power to it and everyone in the room listened to her with rapt attention. It was so quiet there you could hear a pin drop.

Lalita took a special interest in Juanita during the Retreat. She was fluent in Spanish so could speak to Jenny in her native language and she played the violin masterfully between sessions which was Jenny's favorite musical instrument. Lalita's music was original and it touched and opened Jenny's heart. After the Retreat, Jenny learned that she was a trained Christian healer, a Zen Buddhist master and a level-five Shaman. Jenny's life was completely transformed after the Fitzgerald event.

She immediately stopped smoking and effortlessly lost thirty pounds. Toxic foods had lost their attraction to her. On top of that, she became more relaxed, compassionate and understanding in her dealings with prisoners. That's why she approached the jail's tough, old-fashioned warden, Maximillian Rublev, with a proposal. He managed the prison like a military sea captain running a tight ship and his presence was commanding in itself.

"Sir," she said, "I've just completed an amazing Retreat which has changed my entire life for the better. I'm absolutely certain that participating in this Retreat would produce enormous social and psychological benefits for all of our one hundred forty inmates."

Strange as it seemed to her, Rublev *had* noticed some powerful changes in Jenny which he related to and, from the beginning, showed an interest in her transformation.

"Well this matter *does* fall within your job parameters. How much will it cost?"

"The Retreat leader said she'd do it for free for any interested inmate *who sincerely seeks healing*—but she'd need the entire west wing of the prison, including the exercise run, for a week to do it."

"Let's schedule it then," replied Rublev with a straight face, in his usual gruff voice. He was serious.

I'm shocked he agreed to this, thought Jenny.

Chapter 24—<u>Ramon's Recovery</u>

In August of that year, Ramon attended Lalita Fitzgerald's Sweat Lodge. He didn't have to travel far to do it because it was held inside the Wilkinson Road Jail. The experiences he had in that Lodge shattered his dysfunctional patterns of living.

The very presence of a person like Lalita revealed to him a whole new way of being in the world. She was so poised, so graceful and so charismatic that he fell under her spell and followed her every command. And she was tough. Every one of the twenty four hardened prisoners who participated in the Lodge was transfixed by Lalita's personal power. When it was over, Ramon couldn't wait to talk to Roxanne about it. That opportunity came when she visited him on the Sunday after the event.

"She made me fast for twenty-four hours before getting into the Sweat Lodge, Rox. I've never fasted before so I got extremely hambriento—starving in fact.

"What was it like inside the Lodge itself, Ramon?"

"Caliente, very caliente. The place was filled with burning rocks which the facilitator kept throwing water on, producing steam. We had to sweat sitting down in the heat for six hours—naked, painted with red ochre and tied up with hemp ropes."

"Then what happened?"

"She came up to me and pulled the rope tight so that I almost passed out. Then she began to chillari and shout at me en Espanol."

"What did she scream?"

"First she asked if I wanted healing and I said I did—then she made me close my eyes and go back into my childhood and think about my early family life. I started to cry and told her my papa whipped me regularly with a wet bamboo stick. He beat all of us when he got drunk which was almost every day," I told her.

"Close your eyes visualize your padre and imagine you're back with him—do it NOW!" After a long pause she added, "Do you see him?"

"Si, yes I do. He scares me," I cried.

"In your mind go up to him and hug him Ramon and do it NOW", she hollered.

"I can't, I can't I begged her." But she kept yelling at me to hold my dad, kiss him, love him and forgive him.

"He raised you, he fed you, he taught you how to fish and ride a bike, hug him NOW," she ordered while pulling the ropes around me tighter and tighter. Rox—she broke me. I gave up and hugged my papa in my memory and felt love for him. As soon as I forgave him I fainted. When I woke up Lalita splashed my face with a jug of ice cold agua with ice cubes in it.

"Now you can go outside and take a break, Ramon," she said in a soft, compassionate voice. You've earned it.

"When I got outside, everything looked different. The guards seemed like amigos, a bird sitting on the main prison wall looked si bello so wanted to touch it, hold it, stroke it's magnificent wings. I'd stopped thinking and worrying. Everything seemed vibrating with life. Then, during the break, I saw her sitting on a rock outside the prison playing an amazing song en Espanol on her violin. She was smiling at me while she played. Rox—the intense pain in my back was completely gone and I was at peace with myself. I'd become a changed hombre."

After the Lodge was over and all the good-byes were made, Ramon got a chance to talk to Lalita privately for ten minutes. He told her she moved, touched and inspired him and he asked her for an autographed picture of herself, which she unhesitatingly gave him.

"I feel so peaceful in your presence, Senora Fitzgerald," he said. "I'll hang this photo in my cell and pray for continued peace every day. You've saved my life."

"No," she answered, "*You* saved your life—you did the work."

Chapter 25—A Romantic Outing

When Roxanne visited Ramon on Sundays she noticed big changes in him. The wrinkles in his face were gone, he spoke more slowly, he was no longer limping and he always seemed happy.

"I know I can leave the life of drugs now, Rox, and master the welding trade. Maybe buy a casa someday and get married," he said while winking at her. Unfortunately she didn't notice the wink.

"That's wonderful Ramon. This is a turning point for you," she added.

"Yeah, it is, for sure," he added. "How's progress at The Peoples' Place coming along?"

"All the framing is now done and the drywall guys are currently taping walls. The plumbing and electrical work is finished. I think we'll be able to move people in come January."

"Wonderful!" exclaimed Ramon enthusiastically.

The next weekend was Labor Day and she picked Ramon up at the jail early Monday morning. Rosa was with her and they were headed out to the famous country Fair in Saanichton.

"This is Rosa, Ramon—she and I have become very good friends," said Roxanne as they stood beside her Tesla waiting to get in.

"Buenos dias amigas—let's have fun today," said Ramon, grinning like a Cheshire cat. It's mui bueno getting out of that cage." It was a warm cloudless day which put all three of them into a relaxed mode, like butter slowly melting in the sun.

It didn't take Rosa long to notice a romantic flavor to the relationship between her friend and the Latino. They laughed continuously, went on midway rides together and even held hands for a few seconds after the Ferris Wheel ride. Roxanne felt dizzy so she took his hand to steady herself. When they bought just one cone of cotton candy and ate it together, Rosa felt the love and affection in their hearts.

"Rox tells me you go to el templo a lot, Rosa," Ramon stated.

"Yes, it's true—I love spending time at church in prayer—how about you?"

"I grew up Catolica and even sang in the choir. But I gave all that up years ago. When I get out of jail maybe I'll go back. I think Dios is calling me back."

"That'd be a very good idea, Ramon," responded Rosa. "And you could come to my church once in a while—I'd like that."

"It's a deal," replied Ramon solemnly. "I used to pray a lot and maybe I'll return to it."

Later, after they'd left the fair and Ramon was safely back in jail, Rosa told her friend,

"I can see you're really attracted to Ramon and I can understand that. He's a very attractive guy."

"Yes, it seems I am. But the whole scene with him is bizarre. He's definitely not the kind of man I was socialized to be with. He comes from a different culture with a unique way of viewing things. I can't explain it but sometimes it feels like I'm just a pile of metal shavings and he's the magnet."

"A very strong magnet at that," sighed Rosa.

"Overpowering in fact," moaned Roxanne.

Chapter 26—Board Meeting

Ten days before Christmas, Bertrand called an official board meeting. It was held in a newly minted classroom at The Peoples' Place. All five members were present: Bertrand, Roxanne, Reverend Allen, the architect, Ron Gillespie and the Deputy Minister, Michael Dalton. Bertrand called the meeting to order by saying,

"Welcome to our first Board Meeting my friends. As chair, I'm happy to announce this morning that construction of The Peoples' Place is now completely finished and it happened two weeks prior to the scheduled opening and on budget. Our first clients will move in on February 1st. It's important that we meet monthly to keep the Center on track, make sure each one of our stated objectives are being met and ensure that all staff and officials are following the constitution. Today we need to sign all the legal agreements, review the case manager's priorities for admittance of homeless persons and finalize the 2008 schedule of events. Are there any questions or comments?"

"I've reviewed the case manager's priorities and generally accept them. But why will we be admitting only 40% men? Asked Roxanne.

"Our legal advice was clear—men are more prone to violence, illicit drug use and petty crimes," replied Bertrand curtly.

"Yes and we shouldn't be spending any more time discussing this matter right now," added Mr. Gillespie. "It's important that we set a precedent now to follow our own legal advice."

"I can live with a 40% cap on males but 35% would be better. But Ron's right—now's not the time to discuss this in more detail."

The meeting proceeded in an orderly fashion. Roxanne was impressed by the competence and intelligence of all the board members, but she was keenly aware of the loyalty Bertrand's friends had for him and it bothered her. However, she felt calm and poised enough to ask no further questions. Strangely, her attention was on the physical appearance of the room.

The white paint smells so fresh and strong, she thought. *And the furniture and room layout is perfect. This is going to make an ideal classroom.*

However, she paused before signing the final documents because Gillespie and Dalton only seemed to be interacting warmly with Bertrand while tending to ignore her and James. If they did look at Roxanne it was with frowns and knitted eyebrows.

What are they concerned about? She thought. *Somehow it feels like there's already a split in this group.*

Despite her reservations, she eventually did sign all the papers, having quickly scanned them and finding nothing that concerned her. The essential legal structure of the Center was generally acceptable to her and on that matter she trusted Bertrand. She was going to be in charge of the Center's activities, staffing, programs and apprenticeships. Her dream for the homeless was going to happen.

Bertrand can handle all the legal issues, she thought. *I won't have time to do that.*

Chapter 27—<u>Christmas</u>

Five days before Christmas that year Roxanne received a cell phone call from a very exuberant friend.

"Roxy—I'm being released manyana—getting out early for bueno behavior! Can you pick me up at 10 am?"

"Ramon, that's wonderful news—congratulations. Yes! I'll be there tomorrow morning to get you," she blurted out.

She arrived on time the next morning but Ramon was already waiting for her dressed in clean, pressed cotton slacks, a smart khaki jacket, brown oxford shoes freshly shone and a red toque with green Christmas trees all over it. After hugging him tightly, Roxanne said,

"Let's go to Starbucks and celebrate!"

"Ola, yeah—can't wait," he replied.

Roxanne ordered a hot chocolate with whipped cream while Ramon got a coffee loaded with cream, two packets of brown sugar, a double breakfast sandwich with two eggs, three golden hash browns and four packages of ketchup.

"You must have been a model prisoner," stated Roxanne matter-of-factly.

"Yeah and I helped a lot of other prisoneros stay calm. Ever since the Sweat Lodge things have changed. I talk to Lalita's picture every day."

"Do you have a place to stay, Ramon?"

"No Rox—my old amigos have all left me. I'm going stay at el parador hostel downtown for a bit."

"Ramon, you don't have to stay in a hostel—you're welcome to move into my duplex because I'm not living there right now."

"But I can't pay you any rent until I get job."

"That's not a problem. You can pay me when and if you can."

At that point the Latino leaned forward and kissed Roxanne on the cheek.

"You're a true amiga—my best friend."

"That's nice Ramon. Would you like to join me and Reverend James at *Your Place* for a community Christmas Dinner on December 25th?

"Ola! Yes, yes of course. I'll do anything to be with you."

"That's so great. Local furniture businessman Peter Shelton is putting on a turkey meal in the afternoon—with all the trimmings—for the homeless community. He does it every year. I'm glad you'll be there to join me and my friends."

Roxanne was happy to be with Ramon and happy to be helping him out. She didn't bother telling him she was living with another man and having a special Christmas breakfast with that man on the same day as the Shelton event. Luckily, Bertrand wouldn't be able to attend the afternoon homeless function.

Chapter 28—The Opening

As the year came to an end, Roxanne had to deal with some important inner conflicts. She'd fallen madly in love with a transformed Latino but couldn't consummate an affair with him because she was under contract to live with another man. Her dream of directing a multi-purpose homeless center was materializing but in the process she was going to have to deal with potentially hostile members of the Board. Also, her spiritual life was deepening but she worried that the complex responsibilities of managing staff, clients, programs, events and social workers would distract her from contemplative pursuits and quality time spent with homeless people.

Ramon moved into her duplex and was working as a union welder by the middle of January. He wanted to be with Roxanne as much as he possibly could and didn't really understand the excuses she gave him for living away. But the positive changes to his lifestyle, values and activities were authentic and Roxanne found nothing blocking her from being his real partner now that all of his negative qualities had apparently disappeared—at least in theory. The only stressor in his life was a very sick mother who was bedridden in a senior's home suffering from the onset of dementia. Sometimes, she couldn't even remember her son's name.

Roxanne had given notice to her employer for her role as a homeless street outreach worker for Your Place, effective January 31st and was immersed in preparations for the grand opening of the Center. She was focusing on hiring all the staff, creating the apprenticeship programs, designing the cafeteria and liaising with all the Ministry case workers. It'd been determined that the Center's housing priorities were based on: (1st) those who were heavily addicted, had no resources at all and were living on the streets, (2nd) desperately poor people with disabilities who had no other personal or institutional supports and, (3rd) more functional homeless clients who could reasonably be expected to transition back into society within one year.

The People's Place became a functional reality with great fanfare on February 1st, 2008. In attendance at the opening ceremony in the Center's lobby were the city's mayor, all the members of the board, several ministry officials, the local MP and MLA and over one hundred homeless people. Jonas Bertrand opened the ceremony by saying,

"I'd like to open this event by welcoming you all to The Peoples' Place. This Center will be a major benefit to our community in many ways. It will house and feed hundreds of people who are temporarily without a home at this time and offer apprenticeship programs in cooking, janitorial and retail sales which will lead to meaningful careers for many of our clients. Please welcome our CEO, Ms. Roxanne Wilson."

Roxanne stepped up to the podium listening to all the loud clapping with a wide, contented smile on her face and announced,

"Welcome my friends! At long last our multi-purpose Center is open! I'm looking forward to working with you all as we assemble our programs, open up our Thrift Shop and Cafeteria and watch our residential floors fill up with lots of formerly homeless residents. I'll be working with you closely and supporting you fully. My office is on the third floor in the north-east corner facing the back windows and I'll maintain a permanent *open door policy*. That means you can come up and talk to me anytime."

At that point she cut the ribbon strung between two front doors and toasted the assemblage with orange juice mixed with soda water, saying, "Long live The Peoples' Place. Please help yourself to coffee, tea, fruit juice, hot chocolate and all the refreshments laid out before you."

PART 2

DISTRACTION

Chapter 29—Executive Tensions

By the end of March, 2008 all eighty of the residential spaces at The Peoples' Place_had been filled. Roxanne was the CEO of a functionally effective social institution catering to the homeless inhabitants of Victoria. And it was making a big difference to hundreds of formerly destitute people.

However, it seemed to Roxanne that new problems and difficulties cropped up on a daily basis. Several groups of neighbors constantly complained about the noise outside the Center when residents hung out there—smoking, spitting, and swearing. Four inmates had to be ejected in the first few months of operation for stealing and two had died from overdosing on heroin. On top of that, despite Roxanne's power to administer the Center's activities and events, the board passed several policy matters by a vote of three to two that she could barely tolerate. Those included forcing all residents to attend a church service every Sunday, a ban on homosexual clients, instant ejection for any woman who became pregnant and a series of monetary fines for any breakage of the House Rules, many of which were unrealistically strict.

"It makes no sense to ban homosexuality at the Center. What's a person's sexuality got to do with their social position?" Roxanne grilled Bertrand at dinner one evening in late May. Her face was extremely flushed at the time. She was as angry as a caged and hungry tiger.

"I don't really have an opinion on that, Rox—but my two friends on the Board are adamant that homosexuality is unchristian. They really want to keep the Center a godly place."

"That's bullshit, Jonas and you know it. Why do you continually capitulate to those idiot pals of yours? God doesn't discriminate based on sexuality. That's a crazy idea. Actually God doesn't discriminate at all."

"Please calm down, Roxanne, I'm just trying to keep the peace. By the way, all of us on the Board think you're doing a fabulous job of running the place."

"And why is getting pregnant a reason for ejection? Everyone knows two members of the board are pro-life fanatics. One of them told me he couldn't condone an abortion even if it involved rape, incest or the life of the mother. Surely you agree with me that a woman's body must be free from administrative restrictions."

"These issues aren't really that important. Please try to understand and focus on the big picture."

"I just wish you'd grow some balls—that's all," grimaced Roxanne."You don't agree with these policies and yet you're condoning them. That's unadulterated hypocrisy."

Those kinds of conversations began to happen more frequently in the Bertrand household and they accentuated Roxanne's extreme frustration at her lack of ultimate control at the Center. She began to feel like the peanut butter in a sandwich—squished between the needs of her clients and the majority politic of the Board.

These problems were offset by the satisfaction she experienced around the apprenticeship programs, the

Frugal Thrift Shop, the Smiles Cafeteria and the housing of eighty very needy people. They were the successful programs Roxanne had created, administered and guided. The Peoples' Place was truly making a difference.

But the biggest frustration for Roxanne was that she was now spending most of her time interacting with and supervising staff and not working directly with the residents of The Peoples' Place. Many of those interactions were extremely stressful and took her away from the spiritual satisfaction she received from actually helping the actual clients, one-on-one.

Chapter 30—Staffing Problems

Roxanne had hired six employees all of whom received fair wages subsidized by the provincial government. Thereafter, she spent eighty percent of her time managing them.

Terry Springer was the_Institute's_janitor responsible for cleaning the entire complex every day. He was also in charge of managing the janitorial apprenticeship program for qualified clients. At any one time there were up to six apprentices who helped Terry with the cleaning, attended weekly classes and studied all aspects of the trade. It was Terry's responsibility to ensure all his students passed their final exams and were fully capable of holding down a cleaning job after their course was completed. He did an excellent job handling all aspects of his mandate.

Unfortunately, he was prone to making inappropriate sexual advances on female residents that appealed to his virile nature. After receiving two written complaints, certain members of the Board suggested his termination. Roxanne stood up to them and supported Terry.

"Let's appreciate the job he's doing. I know I can turn his offensive behavior around," she stated emphatically at a Board Meeting.

"If it happens again Roxanne, he'll have to go," replied Mr. Dalton, speaking with condescension in his voice.

"I second that idea," echoed Ron Gillespie.

"Do you agree with that edict, Jonas?" asked Roxanne, staring directly at him.

Bertrand responded edgily by saying, "Yes, I do."

"It won't happen again, then." Replied Roxy.

After that she spent countless hours counseling Terry and making sure he knew what would happen if he erred again. Fortunately, he had a great deal of respect for the CEO. As a matter of fact he had a crush on her.

Gillian Macdonald, a qualified Red Seal chef, was hired to run the Smiles Cafeteria. This included creating a menu, buying and pricing the food within a budget and managing the cooks training program. She was allowed to bring a maximum of twelve, formerly homeless helpers into the kitchen to train. That meant she was accountable for her underlings passing the course and finding meaningful employment as a result of the training. She was an outstanding cook and manager; charismatic, smart, attractive and compassionate. Her major flaw was personal time management because she was frequently late for work and often absent for no believable reason. Roxanne had to coach her constantly about this problem. And it was Roxy who had to run the cafeteria when Gillian didn't show up for work.

Jack Turner had a degree in Social Work from the University of Lethbridge in Alberta and experience as the manager of a Salvation Army Thrift Shop in Duncan, BC. He'd also owned a quaint second-hand book store in this youth and sold it for a small profit. He was hired to run the Frugal Shop at The Peoples' Place and train appropriate clients in retail sales. He was an excellent leader and commanded complete loyalty from all his workers. Unfortunately, he had difficulty taking direction from Roxanne. Actually, he had difficulty taking direction from *any* woman.

"My mother wore the pants in my family and that drove me crazy," he always used to say.

On top of that, he was a heavy beer drinker and sometimes came to work hung-over. Luckily he never drank on the job. Roxanne told him that if she ever smelled alcohol on his breath he'd be sent home and written up. His character flaws meant Roxanne had to supervise his operation more closely than she'd have liked.

Liz Carter was the receptionist for the entire Center. She was a friendly, capable nineteen year old who'd graduated from a ten month legal secretary program at Sprott-Shaw College. She had exceptionally good computer skills and even managed a website for her own craft sales. Other than the fact that she had difficulty prioritizing tasks and spent too much time on inconsequential details, she did an excellent job. Everyone loved her. But she did require close management by Roxanne.

Rose Galbraith and Joan Rodriquez joined the team as two experienced, registered social workers. They were responsible for administering the naloxone kits in case any resident overdosed on heroin, morphine, fentanyl, cargentanil or codeine. But their largest mandate was to counsel the residents with special attention to those who were addicted to substances, hopelessly depressed, friendless or lonely. If any problems arose that were *beyond their pay grade* they simply referred their clients to specialized external agencies. With these two professionals in place the complaints from neighbors about unruly behavior slowly began to wane.

However, despite the fact that Roxanne had created a Peer Support Program for Rose and Joan to administer, the two social workers continually requested more programs and funds to assist them in their work. These demands became somewhat of a burden for the CEO.

Roxy brought on Bill Dunhill to serve as the Center's full time security guard. He had to keep the peace, deal with neighbor's complaints regarding rowdy incidents and monitor all the alarms. His essential job was to secure the building and break-up any loud resident conflicts or violent outbreaks and keep the building free of outside criminal activity. As a retired RCMP sergeant he was very capable of handling these requirements and Roxanne was generally happy with his work. But occasionally she had to counsel him not to be so strict and physically tough on her mostly fragile occupants. On one occasion he tripped and pushed a resident who was putting graffiti on the Center's main door. Unfortunately that resident fell to the ground and broke his ankle in the fall. Roxanne made sure no charges were laid but the stress of that catastrophe took a toll on her.

At the end of a long week in mid-July she almost fell asleep driving to Bertrand's after work.

I've got to talk to my mentors about the way life is going for me, she thought as she passed through the gates to her temporary home. *Something's got to change.*

Chapter 31—<u>Mentorship</u>

The following Tuesday Roxanne met with Rev. Allen for supper at Lee's Chinese Restaurant in Esquimalt. Over a combo plate of chicken chow mein, beef chop suey, steamed white rice smothered in soy sauce and Chinese tea she unburdened herself regarding some of the problems and conflicts happening at The Peoples' Place.

She started by stating, "Rev. I'm not enjoying my job right now—actually it's depressing me."

"How can that be, Roxy, amazing things are happening at the Center right now. Your work is really making a difference to hundreds of homeless folks."

"Can I discuss some of the issues that are driving me crazy?"

"Yes, of course—shoot."

"Gillespie and Dalton are turning the Board into a war zone. Do you notice how they disagree with every policy proposal I make?"

"For the most part you're right even though they do sometimes praise your hard work and leadership skills with the staff. But there's no doubt some kind of adversarial role is going on and Bertrand always sides with his two friends."

Rev—those buddies of Jonas glower at me and insult my ideas constantly. On every important matter the vote is always three to two. Thank God you're always on my side!"

"I'll always be on your side, my dear," tactfully added Allen.

"There's something else I want to discuss Rev."

"Go ahead, I'm all ears."

"I'm spending eighty percent of my time babysitting staff and I miss being with those that are disenfranchised. When I was on the street, it felt like I was really helping people on a daily basis. When I saw their suffering first hand I experienced a sense of selflessness. With my heart going out to them there was no space to consider my own petty problems. Now I go home everyday exhausted with a migraine headache, feeling like what I'm doing is meaningless. I'm like a train that's come off its tracks."

"Yes, but *you* hired all the employees. They can't be *that* bad," noted the Rev, smiling.

"They're not bad. Actually, all of them are very qualified at their jobs. Many are doing excellent work. It's just that they need so much personal support from me. I've become a babysitter and I hate that."

"Roxanne—you're doing a fantastic job managing the Place and I'm not the only one saying that. Just look at what an enormous difference you *are* making to all the homeless communities on the South Island. You're like the queen bee in a hive. All the rest of us are just drones."

"Thanks, Rev. Being with you always makes me gain a new perspective."

James Allen is an amazing man. He inspires me, she thought. *Now I've got to talk to Rosa.*

When Roxanne asked if she could talk to her female mentor, Rosa invited her to tea and it was served with fresh homemade raisin bread smeared in organic honey.

After some informal preliminaries, Roxy asked her,

"Can I share some personal and very confidential secrets with you Rosa? I was hoping to get your insights."

Calmly and with poise, Rosa said, "Yes of course and everything you tell me will be kept *our* intimate knowledge only."

"Rosa, I've fallen in love with Ramon."

"You're not telling me anything I didn't already know. Remember, I was with you two at the Fair."

"He wants me to sleep with him—and I'd love to."

"Does he know about your arrangement with Bertrand?"

"No—I just don't have the courage to tell him."

"Roxanne, you *do* have the courage and if Ramon truly loves you he'll understand. I think you have to tell him."

Somehow Roxanne had been carrying on a loving relationship with Ramon for months without him ever knowing why she was living with another man. When he asked her why she didn't come home, her answers were vague and unconvincing.

"Yes—I must tell him what's going on Rosa—he's getting more agitated about this every day."

"May I ask why you aren't making love to Ramon these days?"

"Because my contract with Bertrand specifically forbids any kind of physical intimacy with another man."

"Roxy, it sounds like you're got an inner conflict happening—love versus business."

"Yes, that's true. What do you think I should do?"

"There's only one solution. Spend as much time as you can in deep prayer. Jesus will guide you—that I *do* know."

After her meeting with Rosa, Roxanne started increasing her prayer-life significantly. Even though she was extremely busy at work, she found select times to slip into church, kneel before the figure of Christ and open herself to the deepest levels of her own being. She prayed in bed at night once Bertrand was asleep, every time she went to the bathroom, on short walks in Nature and for moments in her car once reaching a destination. Finally, the answer came.

Chapter 32—<u>Love</u>

Due to extreme exhaustion, Roxanne had fallen asleep in her office right after supper, on a broiling hot August night, 2008.

She dreamt about marrying Ramon. It happened on a white, sandy beach at the Riu Palace in Puerto Vallarta, Mexico. A burning hot sun beat down on the matrimonial gazebo while four Mexican musicians played romantic music in Spanish. Reverend Allen, dressed in full ministerial regalia, eloquently delivered the service. The two hundred guests present could gaze beyond the ceremony onto the gentle, turquoise waves of the Sea of Banderas. Roxanne was wearing a full, long, pure white wedding dress standing beside Ramon who was outfitted in a black sports jacket and colorful salsa tie. Rosa stood beside her—a wonderful maid of honor who'd managed to keep Roxanne calm before the ceremony—and handed Roxy a sparkling, multi-faceted diamond nugget of a ring for Ramon's finger. The bride was in a blissful state at the pinnacle of happiness. At the moment her lips touched those of Ramon she woke up with a start.

"When are you coming to bed? Blurted out Bertrand.

She quickly roused herself and muttered, "Soon Jonas, very soon."

Tomorrow I'm going to tell Ramon everything, she thought.

"I'll be coming over to see you tomorrow night Ramon," she later whispered into her cell phone, outside on the porch behind a palm tree.

"Can't wait querida and I'll have a drink waiting for you."

When she bounded up the steps of her duplex, the first thing she noticed was Snore. He was sitting on the porch balustrade purring, surveying his territory and licking his paws. His whiskers shook when he saw Roxanne.

"Snore, you look beautiful this evening staring into space. Are you looking for a girl friend?

Snore responded by jumping into Roxanne's arms and purring loudly her face.

"Ah," she whispered, "It's good to see you haven't forgotten me."

Ramon opened the door before she knocked and embraced her. Soon they were kissing passionately, both tongues intertwined.

"Ola, my darling, I'm so contendo to see you!"

"Can we sit down and talk Ramon? I've got some important news to tell you."

Si senorita—and I have news for you. But here, my present to you," he said smiling as he handed her a mini, very exquisite purple orchid plant. "You only have to water it once a week but make sure it gets lots of light."

"Thank you so much—its magnificent and I'll treasure it— and thank you for constantly asking me to move back home. I love you and want to do that *now*. But I have to explain why I've been living away. Please try to be understanding.

Actually I've been living with Jonas Bertrand for eighteen months. In order for him to help finance The Peoples' Place he made me sign a contract making me live as his wife for two years. He donated 1.5 million dollars to the project and gave me the use of a brand new car and my own office in his mansion. The contract forbade me from being intimate with any other man or woman.

"Did you have sex with him?"

"Yes—a few times but it was terrible. He's got ED and is an awful lover. Ramon, I only did all this to get our homeless operation off the ground. I believe Jesus wanted the Center to be built. I **do not love** Jonas Bertrand, trust me on that."

"Rox—your shoulders are very tight—let me massage them," stuttered Ramon.

He then placed her in a cedar chair with soft brown leather upholstery—facing backwards. Slowly, he began to rub her shoulders, arms and back. He was right, she was very tight. His hands were supple and strong on her body as it began to relax.

"That feels so good darling," she moaned. "I guess you've forgiven me. So please touch my bare skin now."

Soon she was naked from the waist up and Ramon was sending her into an ecstatic state by touching her with authentic sensitivity. He was, in fact, pouring love into her body.

"I forgive you completely, querida. Relax, the past no longer exists," whispered Ramon.

"Take me to bed now, Ramon. I want to sleep with you all night."

Theoretically she didn't want to break the contract with Bertrand but in this moment she simply couldn't resist the call of love. Ramon kept massaging every part of her body for two hours. After that, every cell in her being was on fire.

"We've had cimar before Rox—but I've never really noticed your entire body. It's magnifico!"

When he entered Roxanne she immediate exploded into a full-bodied orgasm.

"Oh my God—I love you so much," she screamed, "You're amazing!"

Their passionate love-making lasted until 4 am after which Roxanne dozed off into a state of divine contentment and peace.

It wasn't until breakfast that she found out what his news was and it was good. Ramon had just received a promotion at work. He was now a foreman and his salary had jumped 15%.

"That's wonderful news Ramon; I knew you could do it. I'm so proud of you."

"Will you marry me Roxanne," stated Ramon with confidence, staring directly into her eyes. "I mean a *real* marriage."

"Yes," she replied with no hesitation. "Yes I will *as* soon *as you want me to.*"

Chapter 33—<u>Radical Change</u>

The day after her fling with Ramon, Roxanne drove the loaned Toyota into Bertrand's estate and parked it.

She'd arrived at a time her fake husband was working at The Peoples' Place. It took her two hours to pack all her belongings, office accessories and personal documents.

"Here are the keys to the vehicle I've been using, Stricker," she stated with confidence, "And a letter for your boss. Please give it to him. Thank you for all you've done for me— it's been a pleasure knowing you," she said before turning and walking away briskly.

Stricker's face fell in shock as he watched Roxanne exit the property in a Yellow Cab. *The boss is not going to be happy about this, he thought.* Six hours later, on a cold, rainy night after work, Jonas Bertrand read the letter. It said—

August 25th, 2008

Dear Jonas—

I want to thank you wholeheartedly for putting together a deal that launched The Peoples' Place. This Center was my soul's dream and thanks to you, it came true. Unfortunately, I'm going to have to break our contract. The reason is simple: I've fallen in love with a very handsome, charismatic man and plan to marry him in six weeks. Please don't take this personally. I've thoroughly enjoyed working with you and look forward to continuing our business relationship at The Peoples' Place. This is God's work and we're acting as His instruments in making a big difference for the homeless population in our city.

Most sincerely,

Roxanne J. Wilson

Roxanne headed to work the following Monday morning feeling very pleased with the way her life was unfolding. She was finally going to be living with a man she truly loved— someone who was a perfect fit for her. And all her dreams for a homeless Center spanning the entire Island were coming true.

When she arrived at her office, the door was locked. On it was pasted a large brown envelope entitled **NOTICE**. Inside was a legal document which she quickly read—

To: Ms. Roxanne J. Wilson
From: The Board
The Peoples' Place
August 28th, 2008
Message:

In an emergency meeting over the weekend, the Board, in a majority decision, has terminated your employment and business relationship with The Peoples' Place. You will never be permitted on the premises of this organization again. Please note the following paragraph in small print from Section VIII, page 19 in our business contract: "...should the aforementioned party, namely Roxanne Wilson, at any time renege on any of the conditions of this agreement, all her donated monies will be freely awarded to the said organization as a complimentary gift..." No refunds of any kind will therefore be forthcoming.

Your personal and business possessions have been packed and placed in the garden shed adjoining the Wilson Street parking lot and can be picked up any time before midnight on September 4th, 2008. A key to the shed has been temporarily left under its doormat.

Jonas P. Bertrand,
President and CEO,
The People's Place

Part 3

SALVATION

Chapter 34—<u>True Love</u>

Roxanne picked up her boxes and drove home in a state of utter confusion. Once the chattels had been stacked in her garage, she immediately drove to Christ Church Cathedral hoping to find Rosa.

As expected, her friend was deep in prayer alone in the church kneeling with bowed head in the first row of seats, directly under the hanging statue of Christ. So as to not disturb her mentor, Roxanne knelt in the second pew and entered a state of deep prayer.

Dear Jesus, she intoned, *Your will is my sufficiency in all things. I come to You now seeking only clarity and direction.*

Two hours later, Rosa got up and quietly left the cathedral. Roxanne followed her out.

"Can we go to Sonya's for tea?" asked Roxanne.

"Yes, of course."

"Good—I've got something important to tell you."

Once they were seated and sipping green tea, a conversation occurred.

"I'm no longer a CEO at The Peoples' Place."

"Why not; what happened?"

"I got fired today."

"But how could that happen? You were an original investor and the whole project was your idea from the very beginning," noted Rosa.

"Because I got engaged to Ramon, broke the contract with Bertrand and moved back home."

"Oh, my Lord—things happen quickly in your life."

"Rosa—what should I do now?"

"You need to pray and let Jesus guide you. Would you like to come over to may place this afternoon, so we can pray together?"

"Yes, I would," sighed Roxanne without hesitating; noticing that her friend always moved as if in slow motion. She never hurried or did things in a sloppy way. She was always focused in the present moment and all her actions were conducted with an intentionally of precision. There was nothing in authentic about Rosa and in her life there was no moral gray zone. She lived a life of disciplined spiritual intentionality.

At times like this I love being around Rosa, she thought. *This woman makes me feel so peaceful, so calm. Somehow when I'm in her presence, I just* **know** *everything's going to be alright. Her friendship always inspires me to re-focus on all my contemplative practices.*

When Ramon got home after work, he found his lover in the kitchen preparing his favorite meal—beef tacos with guacamole and hot salsa.

"What are you doing home so early, my querida?"

"Ramon, I no longer work at The Peoples' Place. The Board voted to terminate my contract and so they sent me home. It was humiliating for sure because I had to walk out of the building with all my boxes while everyone present just stood frozen, staring at me like penguins in forty below Antarctica weather.

"Mama mia, they can't do that to you querida. You started the place—it was your sueno from the beginning."

"Yes but the Board was always stacked against me and I can't get any of my investment money back."

"Why not? It's **your** dinero!"

"Because the contract I signed had a no refund policy in small print which I never noticed. Somehow I missed that section I signed because I was so excited about getting the Center up and running."

"Does this mean you're broke now?"

"No, Ramon, it doesn't. I still have a savings account, a vehicle and this duplex we're now living in. So don't worry about money."

"I'm not worried querida. Besides, I'm making good money so we're going to be bueno—no matter what happens."

"I love you Ramon."

"I love you too—now let's go to bed," moaned Ramon.

"At 5:30 in the afternoon?"

"Yes."

Chapter 35—Unity

Roxanne Wilson and Ramon Suarez were married on a beach in Bucerias, Mexico on January 15th, 2009. Ramon had grown up in that particular village so many of his old friends were in attendance. For Roxanne, the preceding four months were the happiest in her entire life, for many reasons.

She was living with a man she loved—a man who was handsome, hard-working and virile. A man who treated her like a princess, respected her boundaries, listened actively to every word she spoke and catered to her every need. And despite the fact that she no longer had a job, she continued to minister to homeless people. Spending time with them on a daily basis continued to expand and deepen the compassion in her heart and the development of her spirituality. There were still hundreds of vagrants on South Vancouver Island who hadn't yet been impacted by The Peoples' Place so she had a great deal of work to do any time she wished to serve the plight of the less fortunate. Roxanne had many personal and professional friends and two kindred spirits who'd started out by being her mentors. She'd also grown fond of certain members of Ramon's family.

His sister Maria, who lived in Vancouver, was openly friendly to her and started to communicate regularly with Roxanne via email. She was a voluptuous woman with a very curvy figure who wore low cut dresses and overdosed her skin with cheap French perfume. But the fact that she was a devout Catholic gave them openings for many profound conversations about the meaning and purpose life. Her profession as an active prostitute and drug addict didn't bother Roxanne in the least. She was focused on Maria's character not her occupation or character flaws. And she was always available to help her sister-in-law whenever possible.

Ramon's uncle Emir made her laugh at family gatherings and kept her continually stocked with many varieties of his home-brewed wine. He didn't speak much English and had many sloppy habits but he *did* love to laugh and that sense of humor was infectious. Roxanne was able to ignore his unshaven face, his pot belly, the holes in his pants, his bad breath and his constant puffing on fat tailor-made cigarillos.

Most of all, she loved his mother, Gabriella Gonzalez. Her mother-in-law lived in a nursing home in Victoria and came to dinner at Roxanne and Ramon's place every Sunday night. Although she was old and used a cane to walk she had a photographic memory and noticed everything happening around her. She was smart, talented and sharp as a tack. Her mind was like a steel and well-oiled bear trap.

"Mama's lived a hard life, but she's tough, Roxy—and she's always protected and cared for me, no matter what," Ramon told his new wife.

"Why do you say her life was tough?"

"My madre was married six times and had four children with three of her husband's. She adored and took care of all of us kids. But unfortunately she always chose men who treated her terribly. Three of them frequently beat her and *all* of them eventually deserted her after stealing money from her. She raised all of us by herself—a single parent. Despite that, she made a good living manufacturing and selling special crafts, children's clothes, patch-work quilts and tourist gifts. She also invested in some real estate and became a landlord of sorts which always brought in extra dinero. When she sold a property for a profit she'd take us all on extended vacations. She's fluent in German, Spanish and English and loves to read novels in all three languages. In fact, she taught me how to read and love bueno books. Life was never dull with her. And she was very generous to all her chicos. I'm still very close to my madre and I'll never forget all she did for me growing up."

It didn't take Roxanne long to learn just how close her husband was to his mother. He visited her every day, took her shopping, managed her medical appointments and paid all her bills. Roxanne fully understood and supported his adoration of Gabriella. From her perspective, the marriage to Ramon brought two extended families together in unity and love.

Chapter 36—The Wedding

The ceremony was held on the shores of a beautiful beach with turquoise waves lapping against pearl-white sand. The weather was always sunny and warm at that time of year. Reverend James Allen officiated at the wedding and Rosa served as the maid of honor.

Thirty eight metallic folding chairs were placed in two sections fronting a wooden platform upon which the minister, bride and groom stood. Ramon's sister, Maria stood barefoot in the sand beside the dais and handed her brother an oversized pink-cut diamond ring he'd purchased with the last of his savings. Rosa stood below the platform on the other side and handed Roxanne a shiny, golden, 1.9 carat wedding band for Ramon. When the Rev pronounced them man and wife they kissed passionately for a prolonged period of time. All their friends and family stood up at that point and clapped loudly.

The reception was held at La Riviera Resort—a small pension near the world-famous flea markets. Every kind of popular Mexican cuisine was served along with a wide variety of wines and beers, some brewed by Uncle Emir. The foods included spicy beef tacos, toasted corn tortillas, twisted chicken burritos, fresh avocado guacamole, stewed mincemeat enchiladas and thick, spicy vegetable chilli. At the end of the table closest to the sea stood a two-foot, terraced, angel-food cake covered with silver sparklers and topped by a wedding couple made of chocolate holding hands. All those delicacies took up a great deal of space along the shoreline and nine folding tables were required to hold them. After the meal was served and the cake was consumed, both Roxanne and Ramon said a few words to the gathered assembly after hearing loud ringing sounds from every glass or cup in the room.

"This is the happiest day of my life," stated Roxanne tearily but with confidence, "And I'm delighted you've all come all the way to Mexico to share it with us. Ramon is the love of my life. We're extremely happy together and plan to stay married to each other for the rest of our lives. With all the love and support you give us, this will be entirely possible. I love you all. Thank you again for coming all this way to help us celebrate a very wonderful event."

More clapping and congratulatory shouting ensued before Ramon rose to speak.

"Buenos dais amigos, you are my people! Thank you for coming to our fiesta. There's lots of food and drink for everyone so don't hold back. Then we'll drink and dance long into the night. Please help us celebrate now and have fun. Life is short. So let's dance like no one is watching!" Then he broke out into fits of laughter and started to dance.

For the rest of the wedding week the newly married couple celebrated their union to the fullest. They swam in the ocean, partied with friends and family, ate extremely delicious foods and made love constantly.

"Ramon, I recently lost my job and most of my money but I've never been happier. Promise you'll never leave me," sighed Roxanne after three hours of surfing under a blazing hot sun.

"That would never happen querida. You'll always be the love of my life—I promise."

The only member of the entire wedding party who didn't celebrate excessively, over-indulge their sensual proclivities or drink alcohol was Rosa.

She spent most of her time in St. Augustine's Holy Cathedral which was the only Catholic Church in the village. It was handily located in the middle of the central district, dominating the town's public square. Its steeple was over two hundred feet tall and housed a massive bell that rang loudly every hour on the hour. Inside the building were all seven of the Stations of the Cross, eight towering stain glass windows depicting scenes from the life of Christ, four confessionals which were usually full and a large nativity scene behind the sacristy. There were also several statues of the more famous popes.

It was there that Rosa prayed, confessed, chanted to herself and meditated all day long.

"Rosa, you've got to join some of the festivities or everyone'll think you're a nun," an exasperated Roxanne told her.

"That may be so but I'm doing what makes the Lord happy. Why don't you join me for morning mass?"

Strange as it may seem, Roxanne did just that. For the rest of her vacation she made sure to attend the early morning mass—held for forty-five minutes every morning starting at 6:30. It was strange to see the church almost full that early in the morning.

Catholic Churches don't get this kind of attendance in Canada, she thought

For some time, she'd felt a deep sense of relaxation and peace every time she came into Rosa's presence. And that peace always counter-balanced the usual excesses of a traditional Mexican wedding which she was unable to resist.

Chapter 37—Happy Times

During the winter and spring of 2009, Roxanne felt that her life was finally coming together. Despite the fact she'd lost her job and a small fortune, she still had interest income from two long-term investments and her tenant's rental monthly payment. Her new husband had a good-paying job and was very generous—insisting on buying all the groceries and paying any utility bills that came in. Ramon turned out to be a great cook when it came to Mexican dishes and his wife quickly started to relish his meals. He was also a man who loved animals and they loved him back. He bought a large aquarium, filled it with colored, tropical fish and took very good care of them. Roxanne thought it was good that Snore preferred her husband. Every time he sat down, she'd jump up onto his lap and start purring.

As she deepened her prayer life, Roxanne spent much of her time freely volunteering to support homeless people *on the street*. She got up early four mornings a week to deliver clean clothes, wool blankets, hot coffee and fresh muffins to destitute folks all the way up to Duncan, BC. One morning she glanced at her sleeping husband and felt waves of gratitude. His golden-brown skin, jet-black hair and rippled muscles painted an attractive picture.

How did a woman like me get to deserve such a gorgeous man? she thought.

The new members of her family were well served by Roxanne. She visited her mother-in-law every day to keep her company, administer her medical shots and take her shopping. Maria, Ramon's sister, asked her for counseling.

"I want to leave my life on the streets, Roxy and eliminate all the violence and shit that comes at me every day—but I can't seem to break way," she told her one day.

"What *is* it about your current lifestyle that you *do* like?"

"The money—I make over $5000 a month and have no career qualifications because I flunked out of school in Grade 9. I just couldn't survive on minimum wage today," she answered, frowning. "I've got expensive tastes."

"Can I suggest you join me and your brother at church on Sundays? Perhaps even join our congregation and get back to doing some spiritual work? We have a new minister and she's very dynamic, inspirational and wise."

"But it's an Anglican Church and I'm a Catholic?"

"Maria, that doesn't matter. All Christians worship the same God. Besides, you'll meet many new, wholesome friends there who can show you by their example how to live in a more positive way. Your uncle Emir has even started coming to the Sunday morning service now. It seems like our family's center of gravity has become a church."

"Uncle Emir's a lazy alcoholic and I don't speak to him and haven't ever since he raped me when I was sixteen. I can't even stand to look at him."

"But Maria, your uncle's stopped drinking and he's volunteering at our soup kitchen two hours a week. He's trying to become a better kind of man. And forgiveness is at the heart of Christianity."

Three short weeks later, Roxanne was delighted to tell her husband some good news,

"Ramon—your sister's agreed to join our congregation and now she's starting to pray again. She'll be coming to church this Sunday."

Chapter 38—<u>Potential Challenges</u>

On July 8th, 2009, Roxanne threw a party to celebrate her husband's birthday. It was a barbeque held in her back yard and featured the best Mexican delicacies she was able to create. Their families and friends ate, danced, sang and laughed until it started to get dark.

"Thanks for hiring that Spanish guitarist Roxy," said Maria. "I love dancing to his music. Actually, I love dancing to any music!"

"You're welcome, my dear—he *is* good," commented Roxanne. "This party captures the spirit of a very wonderful, happy family for sure."

"Well I certainly hope that never changes, but I am a bit worried right now," replied Maria.

"Why would you be worried?" asked Ramon.

"Because I saw a fortune teller at the Luxton Fair last weekend, and after staring at her crystal ball for a long time and reading some Tarot cards, she told me dark things were in store for my family this year."

"What dark things?" responded her brother.

"She didn't say. She just scowled and gave me my money back."

"What kind of qualifications did she have? asked Roxanne.

"She wasn't just a country hick, Roxy. She had a degree in psychology and a counselling certificate. She also told me she was born a psychic."

"We don't believe in superstitions anymore Maria, because they're medieval. Her degrees were probably from a mail-order house. Anyway, it's getting dark—let's not think about this anymore. It's time to pack up and end this party."

Two days later, Roxanne's tenant, Charlotte, knocked on her door and handed her a bill for $38. 17.

"It's for rat poison," Roxanne. "I've got rats in my attic and my father told me to use warfarin to kill it."

"Did it work?"

"Yes, absolutely," replied Charlotte. "One small rat died in my kitchen and ended up under the sink. The other one was huge—as big as a cat—and I found it under my bed. It's tail was fourteen inches long and it had fangs like ice tongs."

"That's fine, I'll write you a cheque," replied Roxanne. "Just remember to seal your garbage can and keep any bits of food away from outside your side of the duplex."

Later that evening Ramon was shocked to see the body of Snore lying motionless beside the back yard fence. When he ran out to check on him he found foam oozing out of the cat's mouth and he was as stiff as a board, like a piece of cold concrete.

Roxanne couldn't be consoled. Her beloved pet had consumed a large pellet of rat poison covered in peanut butter and she'd actually paid for the killing substance. Hugging Ramon she cried without reservation. "I truly loved that cat," she moaned.

Chapter 39—<u>Disaster</u>

It took Roxanne two weeks to calm down after she saw Snore lying still in the grass.

"I'm so upset, I don't' even want to hold a funeral service for Snore," she told Ramon. "And I won't get a new cat this time. Losing them is too traumatic for me."

"I can understand that, querida and don't forget I loved Snore too!"

In early August, the newlyweds were sunbathing on colored full-length lawn chairs—lying peacefully while soaking up the hot sun. Roxanne was luxuriating in the heat, admiring the yellow-orange Monarch butterflies flitting between the sun flowers in her expanded garden. She was calmly meditating while noticing how beautiful her husband looked. His hair was jet black, his skin golden brown and his muscular biceps rippled in the sunlight.

When we have sex, he transforms something sleazy and mechanical into a sacred act by pouring all his love into me, she thought.

Suddenly, the silence was broken by the loud ringing of her cell.

"May I speak to Ramon Perez, please?" Stated a baritone voice coming out of the phone.

"Hello," said Ramon.

"Is this Ramon Perez?"

"Si, yes it is, sir."

"It's Dr. Peter Hawkins speaking. I'm an emergency room doctor at the Victoria General Hospital. Your mother's currently under my care and she's not doing well. Can you get here as soon as possible?"

"What's the matter with my madre?"

"Mr. Perez, she fell down a flight of stairs at her nursing home and shattered her right hip. The shock of that injury caused a brain aneurysm and she's now unconscious."

Ramon threw Roxanne's phone into a clump of grass and took off running as fast as he could—like a terrified antelope.

"Where are you going so fast, Ramon?" Queried his wife.

But he was moving so quickly he didn't hear her question.

Ramon spent a week beside his mother's bedside before she passed away. During that time, he read, talked and sang to her but she would *not* wake up. He was distraught. Roxanne brought him food and drink and tried to console him.

"She lived a full life, darling—for ninety six years," whispered Roxanne into her husband's left ear, "And she was happy. She knew you adored her and now we can have a Celebration of Life to honor her and allow her to move on to her next adventure."

But Ramon just kept on sobbing, grief-stricken. His heart was broken, like an egg that had crashed to the floor. And he couldn't understand why neither his sister nor uncle came to visit Gabriella.

His mother's Celebration of Life happened at the Fairview Nursing Home where she'd been living. It was held in the Cedar Room, and twenty-eight people attended—most of them fellow residents. The full Catholic service was led by Monsignor Alcaraz from the Sacred Heart Church on Cormorant Street. Ramon was unable to speak but Roxanne gave a powerful eulogy for a woman she'd come to know and love. Maria attended dressed in torn jeans, a tatty black leather jacket and brown cowboy boots. Both the tattoos on her right arm were very visible. One was a red crab and the other a black anchor. She brought three wilted carnations in a vase and placed them on the welcoming table beside ten photo albums and Gabriella's Family Bible. Uncle Emir came with nothing. He *did* babble a few incoherent words to Roxanne but she couldn't understand them because he was drunk.

Both Ramon and Roxanne attended Sands Funeral Parlor to identify the deceased and Ramon signed off on her cremation. Then they walked along the Esquimalt Lagoon in remembrance of his mother. It was her favorite beach—a place where she always came during difficult times. Ramon read the 23rd Psalm in a brief ceremony at Hatley Memorial Gardens as Gabriella's boxed ashes were lowered into the family plot. It was a very solemn time.

Chapter 40—<u>Descent into Hell</u>

Something shifted dramatically for Ramon after his mother's death. He kept working as a welder, but from Roxanne's perspective, he seemed depressed most of the time. Sometimes he disappeared for several hours in the evening and wouldn't tell his wife where he was going.

"You're smoking dope again, Ramon and its making you sad and tired all the time," Roxanne told him pointedly in late August. "Can I do anything to make you feel better?"

"No querida," he replied morosely. "Did you know that Maria has Stage 3 Hepatitis B?"

"Oh no, I didn't know that. Is she going to survive?"

"It's not likely, Rox. She's on heavy meds but isn't taking the drugs. I don't think she's going to make it. As soon as Stage 4 hits she's a goner."

"That's devastating news, how can I help you my love?"

"Did you know that uncle Emir's been charged with sexual assault? A sixteen year old Thai girl who was cleaning his basement suite claims he raped her. He's currently in jail awaiting trial."

"That's terrible. Do you think he's guilty?"

"I don't know but he's asked me for $5000 to hire a lawyer."

"Ramon, don't worry about that—I'll cover the $5000."

"Do you know what happened when Maria and I met our mama's lawyer and he read us her will?

"No, what happened?"

"Maria was given Madre's condo valued at about $275 000 and all the money in her investment accounts, which came to$117,000. I got the family Bible and ten photo albums."

After a long silence, Roxanne replied. "Ramon, I know why she did that. She knew you'd always be able to take care of yourself but she worried about Maria and didn't think she could make it on her own. Your mother adored you both, but you especially."

"Roxanne, I need to salir to Nanaimo for the weekend. I've just go to get away and think everything over. I can only do that alone at this momento."

"Let me come with you. We need to stick together through the hard times. I'll always stand by you."

"No querida, this is something I have to do alone."

Two days later, Roxanne woke up very early after a restless night and sat down to a breakfast of black coffee and dry white toast. She felt disturbed, uneasy and depleted ater a night of bad dreams. While reading the Times Colonist she came upon a shocking article. It read:

Victim of Late-Night Stabbing Identified

The victim of a fatal stabbing Wednesday night on Main Street in Nanaimo has been identified as Ramon Perez. An RCMP spokesperson confirmed Perez was the man killed in a stabbing just before midnight. A bystander confirmed that he owed his dealer $225 for drugs purchased over the last two weeks.

Several people, including a drug dealer and two other women, participated in the attack confining Perez in a room where they duct-taped him to a chair and beat him, lighting his shoulder on fire and branding him with a hot coin.

Police called the Perez death an isolated incident and said there was no ongoing risk to the public.

No arrests have been made. The Vancouver Island Integrated Major Crime Unit is investigating and asked anyone with information about the stabbing to share it with investigators by calling 250-381-6075.

After reading this news, Roxanne crashed to the floor and passed out cold. Ten minutes later she came to, glanced at the newspaper again and began sobbing uncontrollably.

I'm going to kill myself, she thought. *But before I do **that** I must talk to Rosa.*

She arrived at Rosa's apartment at 6:20 am and knocked loudly on her front door.

"Roxanne—it's so early and you look exhausted. What's the matter?" asked Rosa. "I was just getting ready to go to church."

"Ramon's dead. They killed him, Rosa," blubbered Roxanne as a torrent of tears flowed from her beat red eyes down pasty white, swollen cheeks.

Rosa opened her arms and Roxanne pushed through the door and ran into a tight hug with her friend and mentor.

"I'm going to kill myself, I'm going to kill myself," Roxanne kept repeating—over and over again.

"You're not going to kill yourself—you're going to stay with me until your grief's completely healed."

For the next week, Roxanne didn't leave her friend's apartment because Rosa had created a healing space for her that she did not want disturbed. She dimmed all the electric lights and lit a series of candles all over her home while continuously burning lavender incense.

"Jesus wants you to continue working with the homeless people on Vancouver Island and we need to stay in close contact with Him for a few days. Follow me into the cellar now."

Unbeknownst to Roxanne, there was a sacred room in Rosa's small basement. To get there her sponsor had to open a trap door near her bedroom and climb down a long ladder into a space made to look like a chapel. There Roxanne saw a six foot statue of Christ, a communion table, a candleholder with twelve long white candles and a long, cushioned kneeling platform.

"Kneel down with me Roxanne," whispered Rosa, as soon as they entered the holy room together for the first time. It was dark until Rosa lit all twelve of the candles. "Now we're going to do some visualizations. **Close your eyes**."

Roxanne felt at peace in Rosa's secret prayer enclosure and the weight of the world began to finally slip off her neck and shoulders.

"Have you ever seen a leper, Roxanne?"

"No."

"It's a heartbreaking condition that distorts and deforms by robbing its victims of the sensation of pain. As a result, the afflicted can unwittingly cause terrible damage to themselves. And then their skin breaks out into vicious sores that are extremely contagious and often deadly. Now pause and see Jesus coming down a mountain with crowds following Him. All of a sudden, a leper comes up to Him, kneels down and says, "Lord, if you will, you can make me clean." Watch Jesus in your mind as he stretches out His hand and says to the leper, "I will, be clean." And remember how immediately the leprosy disappeared. Do you see it, Roxanne? Do you feel the presence of Jesus **right now**?"

"Yes, Rosa—I do."

And as Roxanne knelt there, in front of the statue of Jesus and feeling His presence in the room, a shift happened in her being. She completely disappeared as a person and became pure presence. All that existed then was the perfection of awareness in the moment. The character and personality of Roxanne had vanished!

Chapter 41—<u>Ascent into Heaven</u>

Every time Roxanne thought about leaving Rosa's place to take care of her husband's end-of-life affairs, her friend put her through more visualizations. Those contemplations always involved the miracles of Jesus and included the healing of the paralytic in Capernaum, the invalid made whole at the pool of Bethesda after thirty-eight years of paralysis, and the restoration of sight to the blind man at Siloam.

In each case Rosa waited patiently—no matter how much time it took—until Roxanne **felt** the actual presence of Jesus. When that occurred, she experienced a loss of personhood and became immersed in a sea of bliss, peace, energy and joy. When Rosa was convinced, this spiritual discipline had taken hold, she instructed her friend to join her in prolonged sessions of prayer. Those prayers simply involved them becoming totally silent—allowing the work of Jesus to fill them. They said nothing. They just listened while resting in the depths of their own being.

"Roxanne *now* it's time for me to give you an important spiritual insight."

"An insight?"

"Yes, don't give this information to anyone else—keep it confidential, alright?"

"Yes, if you say so."

"Fully accept your grief and pain. **Do not fight or resist it**. Let it be. At first, this'll be difficult, but you must persist. If you can get to a place where you can befriend your suffering and tell it you're prepared to live with it forever—something magical will happen."

"What will that be?"

"The grief will be transformed into an inner ally and give you real spiritual power. Actually, Jesus will do all the work. All you have to do is be silent and trust Him. Can you do that?"

"Rosa, I *will* try."

Presently, after another long silence, Rosa said,

"Roxanne—now it's time for you to go home and resume your regular life. **And do not kill yourself.**"

Rosa, thank you for all you've done this past week. Now I can go forth and resume my life—feeling confident that I'll know what to do.

Later that evening she slipped into her home and went directly to bed. During the night, she dreamt she was walking with Jesus, *assisting Him* as He performed miracles. He was teaching her silently—demonstrating how miracles were performed by showing her how to rest in an infinity of peace within herself and allow the mystical alchemy of healing to occur. This could happen when all the compassion in her heart was released to flow directly into anyone afflicted by the hypnotism of worldly suffering. And when that happened, she disappeared, and pure awareness prevailed.

The next morning she woke up as sunlight streamed through her bedroom window. She could hear the loud singing of sparrows and robins and see the beauty of a maple tree's branches hanging right outside her window. Everything moved in slow motion and vibrated with life. Even the rocks below her window were alive.

After a breakfast of scrambled eggs, fruit salad and hot green tea she went outside to retrieve her mail. The first envelope she opened read as follows:

Dear Ms. Perez—

Be advised that your husband's body is currently being held in the hospital morgue and must be taken away by April 30th, 2009.

Please complete all the forms contained in this correspondence before arriving at our institution.

If there are any questions or problems regarding this matter that we can assist you with, do not hesitate to contact our administration office.

Sincerely,

JR Morrison
Chief Administrator
Royal Jubilee Hospital, Victoria, BC

April 30th is tomorrow, thought Roxanne. *I must go to Sands today to arrange for Ramon's funeral.*

Later that day she met with the Executive Director of Sands Funeral Chapel in Colwood, BC. and an orderly process for dealing with Ramon's body was outlined to her. Sands would pick up the corpse from the hospital and bring it to their offices for viewing and identification. After that, the Hatley Memorial Society would take Ramon's body to their burial grounds and cremate it. Subsequently, a ceremony would be held at the graveside beside the family plot.

Three days later Roxanne attended the Funeral Home and found herself alone in a chapel with Ramon's body lying across a table at the front of the room. He was dressed in a bright red shirt with a black vest over it as well as black trousers and black shiny shoes. His face was perfectly still but made-up to look very handsome. His eyes were frozen, staring straight up at the ceiling.

"Ramon you're the love of my life," she whispered. "I promise you I'll never be with another man. You're my inspiration, my reason for continuing to live. I'll cherish all our memories and every minute of the time we spent together—forever. Wherever you are—please rest and be at peace. I love you."

On April 15th, Ramon's boxed-ashes were lowered into his grave on the lawns of Hatley Memorial Gardens. In attendance were Roxanne and a few of her friends, Rosa, Reverend Allen, the minister of St. Paul's and six of her congregants. It was a warm spring day with a gentle breeze blowing across the graves. The sky was clear. The air was crisp. Roxanne was calm and composed when she gave her eulogy, saying,

"Ramon was the love of my life and his passing leaves a hole in my being. He supported me fully in my work with homeless people. He would have wanted me to continue doing that work and that is what I intend to do. May his soul rest in peace."

Chapter 42—A New Reality

Despite the fact that Roxanne had no job, or any outside obligations, she continued her practice of ministering to the homeless people of Victoria. After waking at 4 am and sitting in silence for forty-five minutes every morning, she consumed a light breakfast of peanut butter on rice crackers, then headed out to deliver hot coffee, fresh muffins and all the necessary extra supplies to those destitute in the streets—items which she paid for herself. Once her rounds were done, she went straight to the Victoria General Hospital to visit her sister-in-law who was slowly dying of hepatitis.

"You're looking much better today, Maria," she'd always say.

"Perhaps but one of my nurses told me I'd never leave the hospital," Maria sighed one day.

"Would you like to recover from this and leave the hospital?"

"Why yes of course, but that's impossible."

"Hold my hands, Maria and relax," replied Roxanne. "Now— look directly into my eyes."

"I feel peaceful all of a sudden," responded the patient.

Roxanne remained silent, looking directly into Maria's soul and, after awhile, she closed her eyes. Twenty minutes later she whispered,

"Maria, you're going to recover fully from this. Go to sleep now. I'll be back tomorrow afternoon. And, by the way—I want you to know that I've neutralized all the black

159

predictions that the psychic gave you at the fair through the art of praying. We're not going to have any more bad news."

Ten days later, Roxanne began noticing a big change in Maria's face. Her skin was getting pinker, her eyes frequently sparkled and she began to smile frequently.

"Dr. Chapman says my liver's growing back, and all the jaundice is gone, and she doesn't know why. She said it must be a miracle."

"That's nice to know, Maria—when will you be leaving this place?"

"As soon as possible," answered Maria, laughing. Her face was by then wet with tears of joy.

Roxanne also visited uncle Emir on a regular basis, usually at least three times a week. On her first trip to see him at the Wilkinson Road Jail, she was surprised by his appearance.

"Uncle Emir, you look exhausted, and you've lost a lot of weight."

"Yeah, it's because I never feel like eating anymore."

"Why not?"

"I'm depressed because I **did not** rape that Thai girl. She tried to extort $1000 from me, and I refused. Two days later, she went to the cops and accused me of the crime."

"Emir, look into my eyes and stop talking for a moment. Did you assault that girl—**yes or no**?"

Once he looked directly at Roxanne, her eyes flashed light beams at him, and he became fixated on her face. After staring straight into her pupils for thirty seconds, Emir replied confidently,

"**No,** I did not do it."

"I believe you, Uncle. Now I can contact your lawyer. What's his name?"

"I just happen to have his business card in my pocket. Here it is," said Emir as he slowly handed her Douglas Haskell's card. "By the way, thanks for paying his retainer."

"That's not a problem, Emir. My family is a top priority for me. Drop this matter now, and I'll resolve it for you. Just relax and be patient.

D. Haskell was a very eccentric professional. His law office was housed in what was formerly a large shed at the back of the courthouse gardens beside the high cedar hedge. His workspace was lined with dusty files, and he had no computers, cell phones, or printers. Apart from Rose Callaghan, his part-time sixty-seven-year-old secretary, he worked alone.

Roxanne was shocked by his appearance during her first appointment with him. He was wearing a plaid, red logger's shirt and had his gray hair tied back in a ponytail. His face was slightly unshaven, and his large blue eyes looked out behind a pair of old-fashioned granny glasses.

"Is there any actual evidence that incriminates my uncle?" she asked him.

"Not exactly," replied Haskell. "Anya Suwan, the young victim in this case, waited two days after the alleged assault before reporting it to the police. There was no physical proof of any kind that might have indicated a sex attack occurred. However, your relative has two previous complaints of sexual harassment registered in his criminal file. They could make his defense complicated."

"I'd like to meet Ms. Suwan. What's her address?"

Normally, Haskell would never permit a stranger to have access to the key witness in his case, but something about Roxanne Wilson persuaded him it would be alright. Her presence had a powerful effect on the lawyer. She was most persuasive during the long periods of silence between her spoken words. That secret personal power also came into effect when she met the young Thai girl.

"You've accused Emir Lopez of attacking you, but he denies doing that," she told Anya. He said you tried to get $1000 from him. Is that true? Before you respond, look at me."

At that point, the girl squirmed in her chair, made direct eye contact with her interrogator and blushed deeply. But she didn't say a word.

"Well, I'm going to give you the $1000 right now, Anya," said Roxanne as she peeled off a stack of twenties and handed them over. "Now look straight into my eyes and answer this question: **Did Mr. Lopez rape you?**" After a long, uncomfortable pause, there was an answer.

"No," answered the girl before starting to sob uncontrollably. "I needed the money to pay for rent."

Four days later, Emir was released from prison, and the charge against him was expunged from his record forever.

Chapter 43—<u>Epilogue</u>

During the summer that year, crowds of homeless people tended to congregate into small groups around Roxanne when she appeared on the streets, even if it was very early in the morning. She'd gained a reputation on the street as a healer. Many of her clients had graduated from the streets after Roxanne had intervened on their behalf.

For ten days, she just listened to Fred and Gert Sawyer after sharing coffee and doughnuts with them. Fred's career as a guitarist had ended when he fractured his right hand, and Gert lost her government job after experiencing long Covid. Because of the illness, she lost her voice and couldn't sing with Fred any more, which ended their run as a successful duet. When Roxanne met them they were living in Beacon Hill Park in a pup tent. She did nothing but pay attention to them and listen to them profoundly in a compassionate way. Soon, Fred was using his left hand to play his music, and Gert fully recovered from her ailments and regained her voice. Two months later, they were back singing and made a CD. Then, they started to make enough money to rent a small apartment. They were so grateful to Roxanne that they gave her their tabby cat. His name was Smarty, and he was highly intelligent. He had a distinctive M-shape on his forehead, stripes by his eyes, across his cheeks, along his back and around his legs and tail. And he had swirled patterns on his body, neck, shoulders, sides, flanks, chest and abdomen.

"He seems to prefer you to us," said Fred one day. "And we've had him for three years and love him but we want to give him to you so you'll never forget us."

From that day forward, Smarty accompanied Roxanne on all her adventures both at home and at work. They soon became best friends, and Roxanne vowed to keep him alive into old age.

Jack Lincoln used crutches to walk due to a failed hip surgery in his youth. But after hanging around with Roxanne for a month, he threw the crutches away, got a janitorial job at the Salvation Army and moved into Army housing on Yates Street. Two years later, he started his own janitorial business, which currently runs a very successful operation with twelve employees. Roxanne pays him well to clean her home weekly.

Roxanne's miraculous work with the destitute continued until she retired after fifteen years on the streets and became a recluse who wrote inspirational short stories. All of them had the same theme—redemption from suffering is absolutely possible.

In July, 2024 a twelve-foot bronze statue of Roxanne was built by Mungo John, an up and coming local indigenous sculptor. It was placed right outside the front door of The Peoples' Place. By this time, Jonas Bertrand had died and his two board member cronies had retired.

Gillian Macdonald, the woman Roxanne had hired to run the Smiles Cafeteria, had become the CEO of The Peoples' Place, and one of her first acts in that capacity was to rehabilitate the name and reputation of Roxanne Wilson. When the statue was unveiled at a small civic ceremony, Ms. Macdonald gave a brief speech.

My friends, we gather here today to honor Roxanne Wilson whose vision, drive, compassion and determination made The Peoples' Place a reality. Her work with homeless people over the years made an enormous difference in the lives of hundreds of formerly destitute folks. She'll always be welcomed at our Center, and her name will be synonymous with the power of love to dramatically affect the lives of others. Please join me and the staff for a reception in the renamed Wilson Cafeteria to celebrate Roxanne's life. She'll be signing copies of her latest book of short stories there which she'll then be giving away to anyone here who wants to read it.

At the reception, held later in the cafeteria, Gillian sat with Roxanne at the head table, enjoying the conversation.

"I always wondered how you healed so many lives, Roxanne, including mine. What is your secret?"

"Gillian—thanks for honoring me today. I appreciate all you're doing at The Peoples' Place in this era. But, to be honest, there is no secret. I learned long ago to just fall back into the depths of my own being and let the flow of life take over. And that was my salvation."

About the Author

 RP Mickelson is a natural-born storyteller, and his tales take many forms: short stories, novels, children's books and lively oral encounters. His first novel, *Stone House*, was published in 2021, and his collection, *Inspirational Short Stories*, was published in early 2023. The first work in the *Mystical Healing Series*, *Lalita's Power*, was published in 2024. This novel, *Roxanne's Salvation*, is the second book in the *Trilogy*.

He lives with his wife in Victoria, BC and has three adult children and seven grandchildren.

While his current passion is the game of table tennis, he loves all racquet sports.